'JAMES R. MONTAGUE', an
writer Montague R. (M. R.
PHER WOOD (1935-2015). H
historical novels, adventure novels, the succe......
of humorous erotica (under the pseudonym Timothy Lea), and
novelizations of his own screenplays for the James Bond films *The
Spy Who Loved Me* and *Moonraker*.

James R. Montague

WORMS

VALANCOURT BOOKS

Worms by James R. Montague
Originally published in Great Britain as a paperback original by
Futura in 1979
First Valancourt Books edition 2018

Published by Valancourt Books, Richmond, Virginia
http://www.valancourtbooks.com

ISBN 978-1-948405-18-8 (*trade paperback*)

Also available as an electronic book and an audiobook.

All Valancourt Books publications are printed on acid free paper that
meets all ANSI standards for archival quality paper.

Cover by David Moscati
Set in Dante MT

Men have died from time to time,
and worms have eaten them,
but not for love.

As You Like It

PART I

CHAPTER ONE

When I used to tell people that I lived on the north Norfolk coast they would always say 'How nice' and begin to quote those qualities for which the area is most justly praised: the sea and sailing, the bracing air, the perfection of the light, the magnificent skyscapes, the wild birds and the sturdy, independent character of the local people. There was a time when I would have agreed with them wholeheartedly.

I first came to the area with my wife. We had answered an advertisement for a cabin cruiser on the Broads and after several days' discomfort and an unavailing struggle with an ancient engine we had eventually broken down at Potter Heigham. As far as I was concerned it was a blessing in disguise. I had not enjoyed our intermittent sorties along crowded waterways and when an advantageous refund was offered I accepted it with alacrity. A chance conversation in a local pub canvassed the delights of the north Norfolk coast and the landlord was able to recommend an inn in a seaside village providing bed and breakfast. I rang up immediately and had no difficulty in securing a double room.

It might be thought that my wife would have applauded my initiative but she was all for cutting our losses and returning to our flat in London. She had not enjoyed the cabin cruiser and held out scant hopes for nine days at Blanely affording more rewarding leisure opportunities. I was more optimistic. I was also aware that my wife would soon find a list of odd jobs for me to do if we returned home. I needed a break from my unexciting job in a quantity surveyor's office and I was determined to have one. I therefore dug in my heels and we drove to Blanely.

The inn turned out to be quite sizeable, providing full board and apparently catering for several other guests. We reserved a table for dinner and then went to unpack our cases.

'The bed is very small,' my wife grumbled.

'At least we'll be more comfortable than on the boat,' I told her.

'That wouldn't be difficult,' she said.

I agreed, and suggested that we take a walk. 'There's nearly two hours before dinner.'

'It's too cold,' she said, 'and it looks like rain.' But she put on her coat and headscarf.

My first uneasy impression was that my wife's fears might prove to have been justified, that any diversion to be found in this place would have to be of our own making. There was a bleakness around us; even the landscape looked empty. Blanely is not on the sea itself but tucked away behind a fringe of marshland that runs along the coast and is sometimes flooded at times of high tide. To get to the sea we had to follow a path across the dykes and the salt pools along a high, man-made mound forming a buttress against the sea. Gulls and terns cartwheeled overhead and a brisk northerly wind forced the reed beds into flat, shimmering movement. From the marsh the sea could only be seen as a distant grey swathe and looking back to land the village was a tight-knit huddle of houses silhouetted against the sky like the pop-up illustration in a book of fairy stories. There was no real height to it but it seemed like a miniature Mont St Michel against the interminable flatness of the marsh.

The path itself made several brisk changes of direction before arriving at a sluice gate which marked the point of entry onto the beach. Here one could look down and see small crabs stealthily picking their way upstream through the clear water. Grass gave way to sand and the path debouched into an open area flanked by sand dunes. Beyond them lay a wide beach that stretched away into infinity on either side with scarcely a soul on it. We had taken our holiday in late autumn to avoid the rush but it seemed doubtful if at the height of the tourist season such a beach could ever have been crowded. There was a wild, untamed quality about it.

We crossed the sandy barrier of the dunes with the spiky grass trembling like the lances of an army and I suggested that this would be a good spot to bring a picnic. Amongst the dunes one was well sheltered from the wind and the autumn sun was almost warm. My wife dismissed the idea. She had already started complaining during our walk along the sea wall and I soon saw that she did not share my sense of mounting pleasure in the scene about us. She said that it was far too bleak and baulked at my idea of a walk along the beach. Nevertheless I strode on and she had no alternative but to follow, objecting as usual that she was wearing the wrong shoes. The beach was a treasure trove of shells and coloured stones pounded into a skin-like smoothness by the sea. There were spars and fragments of old lobster pots, green bottles with labels in a foreign language that I thought might be Russian, even the staves of a barrel. I felt that I could walk along this beach all day making up stories about the objects that I found. Every day would bring something different. I revelled, too, in the power of the sea: the comber of pounding waves, the thump and roar as they broke on the beach, the hiss of the receding water. The fragments of man-made things that I came across testified to its power and I loved the noise it made mixed with the high-pitched shriek of the wind. After a while it became almost soothing.

That night I lay awake in our cramped double bed in the inn and listened to the distant sounds of the sea. My wife was asleep and snoring softly. Moonlight streamed through the parted curtains and I was in that delicious state between sleep and wakefulness when one's mind glides easily with the option of drifting into sleep always available. It suddenly occurred to me that I would like to retire to a place like this. My wife had come into a small legacy and we had discussed buying a bungalow on the south coast without the idea ever holding much appeal for me. I could see myself being drawn into the company of other retired couples whom I did not really care for and the whole thing becoming a tedious ritual of whist drives and gossip – perhaps my wife was right when she said that I was basically anti-social. Here, on the north Norfolk coast, there would be no enforced conviviality; one could lose oneself in the wide open spaces or take part in whatever was going on as one felt inclined. I fell asleep resolved to explore the possibilities before we left Blanely.

Most of the other guests at the inn were men on a golfing holiday without their wives and it was their habit to eat early and noisily and depart to the nearby links. We soon got the measure of their behaviour and came down later when the small breakfast room was empty and there was no need for the exchange of tedious civilities. On the morning in question I sliced the top from my boiled egg and debated how to broach the subject: best perhaps to test the temperature of the water.

'I saw a pretty little cottage up the road that seemed to be for sale,' I said calmly, inserting my spoon into the yolk. This of course was a fabrication.

'Very likely,' sniffed my wife. 'Somebody moving to somewhere warmer.' She shivered. 'I think this must be the coldest place I've ever been to in my life.'

This was not a promising beginning but I pressed on. 'Still, it's very unspoilt.'

'There's nothing here to spoil,' she said firmly. 'I like a few hills myself. I couldn't stand this flatness all the time.' My heart fell. There it was, spelt out unequivocally; there was no point in making my feelings more explicit. My wife wiped her mouth with her napkin. 'What are we going to do today?'

'I'd like to go for a walk along the beach,' I said.

She shook her head. 'Then you can go alone. I'm not dragging myself out there to freeze to death. The landlord was saying that a bit more goes on at Hunstanton. We could drive there and have a look round. Maybe there'll be something on at the cinema.'

'You go, dear,' I said. 'I think I'll take some more air. I find it very bracing.'

This amounted to a minor rebellion as far as I was concerned and my wife was not pleased. She repeated her demand to go to Hunstanton and made it clear that she would take it ill if I did not accompany her. Nevertheless I stood my ground and, keeping my voice down and my temper under control, I said that there was no reason why we should do everything together and that I would meet up with her in the afternoon or whenever she chose to return. She departed in a high dudgeon.

I was pleased with my show of defiance and continued to sit in the breakfast room reading an old magazine until she had driven the car away, grinding the gears in her anger. I then went upstairs, put on my coat and went out.

This time I made a short tour of the village before retracing my steps towards the sea. In fact I could only see one house for sale and that a modern bungalow set back from the main road – not the kind of property I was seeking. However, I made a note of the agent's name and address and began to walk through the churchyard towards the sea wall. It was a fine church like so many in Norfolk and the lichen-covered gravestones paid tribute to the longevity of the inhabitants. My off-the-cuff remark about the bracing effects of the air must have been correct. A bicycle was leaning against the porch and, as I approached, the vicar emerged sporting a pair of bicycle clips and a vase of dead flowers. We got into conversation and I learned that this was but one of three parishes that he was responsible for. He bemoaned the small congregations and the lack of people prepared to help in the work of the church.

'A marriage, a christening, a death – that's the three times most people come to church these days,' he said. I sympathized and accepted his invitation to look round the church. There was a fine rood screen and a handsome font with figures in painted relief but the *pièces de resistance* were two life-size effigies carved in stone, lying side by side on tombs with stone dogs at their feet. Their ruffs and doublets placed them as a sixteenth-century couple and I admired the intricacy of the carving and the design on the sides of the tombs. One unusual feature of the motif was what I first took to be either flames or snakes writhing upwards towards the two bodies.

The vicar corrected me. 'The worms of hell,' he said. 'They rear in pursuit of the souls of the deceased.'

I nodded, thinking it a macabre idea, and turned away from the fakir's bed of worms. The temperature of the church suddenly seemed to have dropped several degrees; the cold was so severe that it almost took the breath away. The vicar rubbed his hands together and without another word, both of us strode down the aisle and came out into the open. 'It suddenly seemed cold in there,' I said.

'Yes,' said the vicar. His expression tightened and a look of distaste came over his face as if I had touched upon an awkward subject. There was a short exchange of banalities and he climbed on his bicycle and creaked away without looking back. I was probably exaggerating but I felt that the downward pressure he exerted on the pedals suggested a desire to put as much distance between the church and himself as possible.

I went through a lych-gate and followed the path along the sea wall. The wind was blowing strong and the few trees around were permanently leaning away from the sea, their branches gnarled and spread like the fingers of arthritic hands. They seemed to be raised in a gesture of self-preservation against the elements. Once again I filled my lungs and enjoyed the power that was being unleashed all about me. Battalions of clouds broke and reformed high above my head as they sped inland and there were distant menacing patches of black as if a storm was on its way. My raincoat was flapping round my legs and I felt exhilarated, ready for anything that nature could throw at me. When I reached the beach the sky was dark and the wind had dropped to an eerie whisper that rustled the coarse grasses on top of the dunes. I was annoyed to find that I was not alone. Beyond the first bank of shingle a man was digging in the sand. As I watched, he bent down and plucked something up before dropping it into a bucket. He must be digging for bait, I thought – ragworms or the like. For a second it flashed across my mind that this was my second exposure to worms within the space of half an hour but I attached no importance to it.

I started to walk along the beach in the shadow of the dunes and the man raised himself and saw me. He leant on his spade and gestured towards the sky. 'If you're looking for a soaking you've come to the right place. That sky's going to pour buckets within the half hour.'

I mumbled a response and continued on my way. Some of the mood of defiance that I had shown towards my wife still rested with me; I did not want to turn tail and go back the way I had come. I looked back and saw that the man had taken his own advice. His spade was over his shoulder and he was trudging back towards the dunes. Ahead, the beach curved away into infinity and a weatherbeaten sign reared up like a gibbet. It said, *'Blanely Point Nature Reserve. This is a protected area. The taking of eggs is prohibited.'* I walked on and short sharp squalls of wind began to tug at the tussocks of grass. The sky was dark and lowering. I had the impression that it was slowly descending on the land like a huge black cloak. For the first time I began to feel that my idea of a walk had been foolhardy; everything suggested that I was going to be soaked to the skin at the very least.

Suddenly a spot of rain hit me forcefully on the top of the head, then another. The ground in front of me began to be polka-dotted with dark spots contrasting sharply with the near white of the sand. Then the skies opened and within seconds I was saturated. The rain fell in a continuous downpour like water gushing from a broken gutter. I could see the sea as through opaque glass, and gusts of wind whipped the rain into strange patterns across the sand like the footsteps of a running man, an invisible man. Spurts of sand would rise in the air for a distance of twenty yards or more and then veer sharply to the left or right before disappearing, as if whatever had made them had been snatched heavenwards. Small rivers quickly became torrents as they ran down from the sand dunes.

Had I been properly prepared I might have enjoyed the storm but my lightweight mackintosh and casual shoes and trousers were no match for the elements. Rain ran down my neck and my soaked clothing clung to my body. I was shivering, and wriggling my toes to stop them from freezing. Desperate to find shelter I turned towards the dunes and soon found myself up to the knees in clinging sand. There seemed to be no place where one could escape the combined force of the wind and rain. For a few moments I worried seriously about the dangers of perishing from exposure; I had never been so cold and wet and the downpour showed no signs of diminishing. It was vital to keep moving but I was not used to physical exercise and my supplies of strength were quickly evaporating. I felt that if I lay down I might never get up again. All this may seem like an over-dramatization of my situation but it was exactly how I felt at the time. I was genuinely frightened.

I struggled on through the dunes and the veil of rain and was relieved beyond measure when I suddenly saw a man-made structure looming up before me: a grey outline that I recognized as an old World War Two concrete bunker raised to defend the coast against the threat of German invasion. It was low and squat with recessed apertures widening to provide the maximum field of fire. Sand had piled up against its sides and there was a low rectangular opening which served as an entrance.

I stumbled forward and half-crawled into the bunker. Although protected from the wind and rain I was no warmer and my nostrils told me that the bunker had found use as a latrine. Old tins and scraps of soiled newspaper littered the cement floor and I felt depressed that it had been necessary to take refuge in such a place. I slapped my arms about my body and peered out through the apertures waiting anxiously for any sign that the storm was abating. How my wife would have laughed if she had seen me. She was probably watching the downpour from the comparative comfort of a seafront café in Hunstanton. She would be having a cup of tea and enjoying a cake, the largest and most fattening that the establishment provided. She always ate when she was angry and then blamed me when she put on weight. I began to feel quite irritated myself as I compared my situation to hers. My teeth were chattering and my feet seemed to be frozen to the inside of my shoes. The discomfort of my wet underclothes clinging to my body was intense. I must get back to the inn before she returned and try and find a way of drying my clothes. I could just imagine her self-satisfied voice uttering the words 'It serves you right!'

On the wall somebody had scrawled a skull and crossbones and the word 'DEATH!' For some reason the sight made me grit my chattering teeth and clench my fists. It was almost as if the graffiti was a sentiment expressed against my wife with which I violently concurred. I stamped my feet and as if at a signal the force of the rain began to abate. I could see the glistening dunes and the grey vengeful sea topped with white breakers. The wind still whistled sullenly but the sky had lightened and was now a uniform grey. Since I was already soaked to the skin there was little point in staying where I was; I might as well get back to the inn as quickly as I could. I took a last unloving look round the bunker and ducked out into the open. A mean rain stung my face but the wind had lost its terrifying power. My footprints through the dunes had been completely washed away and the cold cut me like a knife. I needed to get back to the inn by the quickest route possible. Shivering uncontrollably, I hauled myself up to the top of one of the dunes and looked inland. The church tower was clearly visible and in the foreground I noticed what seemed to be another sluice gate, built across a fairly substantial tidal dyke. It was impossible to see clearly but I had the impression that a path ran from the sluice towards the village. If it did so it would certainly provide the short cut I was looking for and

I hurried down the dune talking out loud to propel myself along. I would have made a strange spectacle if there had been anyone around to see me.

The sluice gate was constructed with blocks of concrete, and a metal rail half-eaten through with rust ran along one parapet. The ducts were choked with sedge and timber and I had the impression that it had long since ceased to be used. I was hurrying across with my hand on the rail to steady myself – the concrete being slippery – when one of the metal uprights gave way. I nearly fell. I stumbled sideways against the concrete rampart and experienced an immediate stab of fear. A huge block trembled as I collided with it and for a second I thought that it was going to topple over, taking me with it into the fast flowing water – the tide was coming in with the power of the storm still behind it. I pulled myself up carefully and gingerly pushed against the concrete block. It was definitely balancing precariously and only needed a shove to come crashing down. With that and the faulty rail and the slippery surface under-foot a serious accident was a definite possibility; I would have to report the hazard when I got back to the village. Somebody could be killed.

Now that I look back I find it difficult to remember if the idea occurred to me then. Perhaps only the vague possibility entered my mind: it might have been my wife crossing the sluice instead of me; she might have stumbled against the loose block, bringing it down on top of herself, being crushed beneath it in the mud and sand at the bottom of the dyke. I recall looking down into the dark churned-up water and seeing the particles swirling like clouds. I think I even climbed over the parapet onto one of the long bastions that divided the stream, and pushed at the concrete, testing it to see if it would fall towards the rail. Perhaps this did suggest a measure of pre-meditation. It is difficult to say now when so many things have happened.

When I got back to the inn I was depressed to see the car standing outside it. It was soon revealed that my wife had driven away in such a precipitous hurry that she had left her purse behind. Her reaction to my bedraggled state was everything that I might have expected – I was scolded for making more work for her on what was supposed to be a holiday and for my selfish inconsiderate behaviour generally; it would serve me right if I caught my death of cold. I bore all this and again managed to control my temper. I think that what I had seen at the sluice gate had made me feel that I had a source of hidden power that I was holding in reserve, a kind of ace up the sleeve.

I said that she was right about catching cold and that I ought to go and buy some aspirin to be on the safe side. There was no chemist in the village so I would take the car and go to the nearest town. My wife then began to chide me and say that I was a hypochondriac. The continuing vehemence of her attacks was beginning to get on my nerves.

I picked up a packet of aspirins at the village store and drove to the estate agent whose address I had seen on my tour of the village. It was approaching one o'clock when I got there and I hoped I would find him still open, it being the town's half day. The business was in a shabby side-street off the main thoroughfare of the town and a quick glance at the bungalows offered for sale in the window was not encouraging. I turned my eyes away from the grubby pegboard and pushed open the door. A girl with badly dyed blonde hair was pulling the cover over a typewriter. She did not look pleased to see me, a fact she emphasized by looking at her watch. Before either of us could speak, a man of about fifty came through from the back of the shop. His clothing was not that of a typical estate agent. He wore a quilted waterproof hunting jacket, waterproof over-trousers, and Wellington boots with the tops turned down. A glance at the fishing tackle lying on top of one of the desks told me that he was preparing to shut up shop and go off on a fishing trip. The girl looked at him hopefully and he nodded towards the door.

'All right, Sylvia. I'll look after this gentleman.'

Sylvia picked up an anorak that seemed to be made of the

same material as the typewriter cover. 'See you tomorrow then,' she mumbled as she went out.

'We were just about to close as you can see,' said the man. 'What can I do for you?' He was looking me up and down and I suppose that in my crumpled corduroy trousers and fisherman's jersey – my normal clothes were still drying of course – I must have seemed an unlikely prospective purchaser.

'I'm staying at Blanely,' I said, surprised at how easy it was not to mention my wife. 'I wondered if you had any cottages in the area.'

The man pursed his lips as if I had mentioned a rajah's palace. 'Very sought after little spot, Blanely,' he said. 'Very salubrious. A lot of money about. Very handy for the golf course and the yachting. When something comes on the market it's gone in a flash. We get a lot of people from the Midlands.'

'I can imagine,' I said, already beginning to feel suitably discouraged. 'I wasn't looking for anything large.'

'You're lucky as it happens,' he said, quickly rifling through the sheets of paper on his desk. 'I've got a very nice little property here – very handy for the shops, easy to maintain. You could let it in the summer if—'

'Not Dunrovin,' I interrupted firmly. 'I saw that when I was looking round the village.'

The man's hand faltered and he slowly lowered the piece of paper. 'It's very nice inside,' he said. 'Very attractive wide brick fireplace. It's had a lot of money spent on it.'

'I'd like something with more character,' I said. 'One of those old flint cottages.'

The man pursed his lips at my presumption. 'Now you're asking for something. They fetch the earth when they come on the market.' He quoted a figure that was three times what I had considered paying. 'Even barns and suchlike are being snapped up for conversion. I sold a windmill the other day.' He started to arrange the papers on his desk and I could see that he judged that the interview was over. 'If you'd like to leave your name and address I'll put you on our mailing list.'

I looked down at the desk and wondered what to do. As I did so, my eye lit on a round tin that once might have held tobacco. Some irregular perforations had been made in its lid and through one of them a bright red tentacle suddenly darted into the air like a snake's tongue.

'Wait a minute. I may have something that might suit you,' he said and I looked up. 'A lady who has a property at Blanely wants to sell off one of the outhouses. I believe it's very dilapidated – she says so herself. I've got the letter here somewhere. Haven't had time to catch up with it . . .' He started to shuffle the papers on his desk and accidentally dislodged the tin, which started to roll towards me. I could easily have stopped it but for some reason I felt a repugnance to touch it. Almost mesmerized, I watched as it trundled towards the edge of the desk. At the last second the estate agent saw it and shot out a hand. Too late. The tin brushed his fingertips and fell to the floor. As I looked down it burst open and I started back in distaste. I was looking at a writhing mass of small red worms.

I had always found worms disgusting and these were especially so. Their movements were agitated and at the moment of release they reared up like miniature snakes reacting to an attacker. Furthermore they did not remain in a coagulated mass but immediately began to separate and wriggle away as if they had engineered their own escape. The tin had fallen on a strip of ancient carpet and it was remarkable how the worms were able to insinuate themselves between the fibres and melt from view.

Still overcome by abhorrence I did nothing, and it was the estate agent who let out an oath and sprang round the side of the desk pulling on a pair of heavy gloves. Clumsily he scraped up those worms that were still visible and pressed them back into the tin, crushing down the lid so that some of them were cut in half. The severed ends writhed frenetically, flailing from side to side. Gruesome as the sight of them was, I could not tear my eyes away. The man raised his foot and stamped down hard and repeatedly, covering the area of the carpet where the tin had fallen. Small dark circles began to appear and there was a pungent odour that made me feel sick. After a flurry of motion he stopped stamping. He was breathing hard and his plump face was shiny with sweat. It was easy to see that he was ruffled by what had happened and my own repugnance must have been obvious.

'They're little devils,' he said, clearly feeling that an explanation was necessary. 'They make marvellous bait but you don't want to let them escape.'

'They seem very lively,' I said.

'Yes,' he said. 'We get a lot of them around here. It's funny, up the coast you'll hardly find one.' He placed the tin carefully in the bottom of a haversack and pulled off his gloves. The stench in the office was now overpowering; more than anything I wanted to get out, to breathe the fresh air, and I made for the door.

'Here we are.' He picked up a letter. 'Mrs Valentine, Marsh House. Anybody will be able to tell you where it is. Tell her I sent you of course ...' He scribbled the name and address on a business card and brought it over to me. I noticed that he scrawled 'Price to be resolved' under his signature. 'Get in touch again if you're interested.'

I said that I would and took my leave. The prospect of finding a house now seemed of secondary importance compared to getting away from that revolting smell and the recollection of those disgusting, writhing creatures. I thought that I glimpsed another on the floor as I opened the door to the street, but I did not look down again to confirm the impression. I hurried to my car and drove back to Blanely.

CHAPTER TWO

My wife was not glad to see me. Much of the golf course had been flooded by the downpour and with greens turned into pools there was little hope of any more play during the day. The golfing fraternity had therefore returned to the inn and were now making a great deal of noise in the saloon bar. In a corner of that same bar my wife was toying with a beef and pickle sandwich washed down by tiny sips of gin and lime. She complained about what she called the 'uproar' and the unsavoury jokes, above all, about the fact that I had kept her waiting for her lunch. On all counts I was the sole recipient of her grievances. It was made clear to me that I had a lot to make up for and as this message sank in it soon became obvious that I was not going to be able to escape twice in the course of one day. I would have to put off a visit to Mrs Valentine's property.

My wife had another gin and lime and a Tia Maria with her coffee and after a nap was sufficiently restored in spirits as to wish to be taken back to Hunstanton. There I dutifully drove her and we walked along the front, past the closed amusement park and an ancient pier wrecked by storms and crumbling into the sea. The wind was brisk and I noted that there were few other holidaymakers in the town. Many hotels and cafés had shut and a run-down, end-of-season atmosphere prevailed which I found depressing. We had an indifferent tea in a residential hotel and the loudest sound in the room was the ticking of a grandfather clock. I thought about what the estate agent had described as an 'outhouse' and felt a mounting sense of anger against my wife that I could not go there and view the property immediately. Supposing somebody else came upon the scene and bought it whilst I was dallying? It was an unlikely prospect but it helped stoke my brooding frustration.

That night I lay in bed and again listened to the sea. It might be thought that after my experience on the beach my enthusiasm would have waned but this was not the case. Sharply defined images thrust themselves into my mind; I pictured the windswept scene, the quietness and austerity of the landscape. I felt peculiarly elated, as if my senses were coming awake for the first time. I looked towards the window and saw the curtains trembling in the wind. They had a nondescript pattern of coloured vertical lines but now as they shivered transparently I could see the same design as on the side of the tomb in the church: the worms of hell. In a quick subliminal flash, I saw the old man on the beach, his gleaming spade coming down like a guillotine as it dug into the wet sand. Then the severed worms dancing. I sat up and shook my head. This was not like my dreamless dozing of the previous night. I was being menaced by recurring images.

I turned and shuddered as I saw a wisp of hair lying across my sleeping wife's forehead. She twisted and the hair fell to curve into her ear, as if trying to enter it. I took a deep breath and turned away. I had to learn to control my imagination. There was no reason to think what I was thinking. If I shivered it must be because I was cold. I reached across to move the lock of hair aside and she twitched in her sleep and brushed my hand away. It was an involuntary gesture but perhaps all the more distressing for that; it was as though her rejection of me was automatic and instinctive. I lay back and avoided looking at the curtain. Black thoughts always arrived at night; it would be better in the morning.

The next day I was woken by car doors slamming as the golfers set off for the links. Sunlight streamed through a gap in the curtains and when I looked at the harmless and rather ugly pattern of red, green and blue lines I smiled at my anxiety of the night before. The only worms around would be harmlessly throwing up casts on the lawn and listening for the approach of predatory thrushes. I could sense that my wife was in no mood to get up early and I rose and dressed whilst she quickly moved into the part of the bed that I had vacated. 'I'm going for a little walk, dear,' I said. She made no answer and I raised the latch and went down the creaking stairs.

The landlord was surprised to see me up with the golfers and jokingly asked if I was on my way to the links. We exchanged a few words and I asked him for the whereabouts of Mrs Valentine's house. It was apparently up the other end of the village, near the mouth of the estuary, and I could see him looking at me questioningly; he wanted to ask why I required such information but he said nothing, and I merely parted with the observation that I hoped the good weather would last for the rest of our stay.

After a brisk walk that took me past the few shops in the village, the methodist chapel and the constable's house, I came to a row of Georgian cottages and beyond that a line of elms that had mercifully been spared from the Dutch elm disease. I could see a small park with horses grazing in it, and over the tree tops the grouped chimneys of a substantial house. On the far side of the house was the open marsh and the sea. I approached the gate and hesitated, wondering whether to proceed up the drive. It was still not nine o'clock and perhaps dauntingly early to call.

I was spared from making a decision by the appearance of a handsome woman of advanced middle age. I judged that she was the same age as myself, perhaps in the early or middle fifties. She wore a tweed skirt, a golfing jacket and brogues and was clearly bent on walking the two elderly King Charles spaniels that accompanied her, their chins almost resting on the ground. She looked at me inquiringly as I stood poised in the gateway and I smiled as agreeably as I was able.

'Am I by any chance addressing Mrs Valentine?' I asked.

She assured me that I was and I went on to produce the estate agent's card and announce the purpose of my visit, apologizing of course for my early arrival. She said that this did not matter and retraced her steps up the drive with me in attendance. It was her turn to talk and she explained that she had been fairly recently widowed and was now finding that the upkeep of a large house made substantial inroads into the income she derived from her late husband's pension and insurance arrangements. Looking around the garden I could see at a glance that it had been neglected; shrubs and plants were straggly and overgrown and weeds choked the flower-beds. She followed my gaze and confirmed that a permanent gardener had had to be replaced by an odd-job man who came in a couple of times a week. I sympathized and waited in the drive whilst she went inside the house to get the keys. It was a splendid Georgian building but badly in need of a coat of paint.

When Mrs Valentine reappeared I could not help noticing that she had applied some powder to her nose and cheeks and tidied her hair. I was flattered. We walked along a path, with a box hedge on one side and an old red brick wall lined with plum trees on the other, and approached a building that once might have been a stable. It was situated exactly at the corner of the property, looking out across the marshes to the sea and positioned a hundred yards or so from the house. The windows were green and dirty and a bramble almost covered the door. Part of the roof had fallen in and I could see blackened timbers. Mrs Valentine saw my worried face and misconstrued my expression. She thought I was horrified by what I saw, whereas I was in fact delighted by the situation of the building and could see its possibilities. What made me appear anxious was the thought of my wife's reaction. I could almost hear her scornful disbelief if I told her that I wanted to spend her legacy on what she would clearly believe was a ruin.

'My husband used it as a workshop,' explained Mrs Valentine. 'Unfortunately a window blew open and the wind caused a paraffin heater to flare up and set fire to a curtain. As you're going to see, I'm afraid the interior was badly damaged.' Her tone was openly apologetic and she was obviously far from being an experienced saleswoman. I could imagine the estate agent crooning over the possibilities of the place if he had not been too busy with his fishing. The key turned in the lock with difficulty and I stood aside to let her enter ahead of me. A slight blush illuminated her cheek as she passed through the doorway followed by the dogs.

Inside, the air seemed to be colder, and I saw that the roof was exposed to the heavens; above our heads most of the floorboards were either burnt or rotted away and the brick floor heaped with debris. Evidence of its original use as a stable was visible in the stalls and mangers but a handsome brick fireplace dominated one wall, perhaps originally installed for the comfort of the grooms or, more probably, the health of the horses. A work bench and tools stood against one wall and there were shelves of paint tins, brushes and bottles of turpentine now covered in rust and cobwebs. It looked as if Mr Valentine had abandoned all interest in the place after the fire. I saw Mrs Valentine looking at me nervously and for this reason allowed my face to set into an even gloomier expression.

'I'm afraid it is in an awful state,' she said.

'Yes,' I said, tight-lipped. I crossed to one of the windows that looked out over the marsh and rubbed some of the dirt from the pane. It was a fine morning and the view was splendid: the sea about a quarter of a mile away with nothing between it and us but the marsh, the mudflats and the sky. Small birds were chattering in the rushes a few yards from the window and as I watched a flight of ducks flew overhead and out towards the mouth of the estuary. I could see the serpentine coil of the river as it wound inland and the glistening muddy banks revealed by the low tide.

Nearer at hand was a deep channel that seemed to lead directly under the building. Its sides were smooth and slippery but there was less than a foot of water in the bottom which suggested that it must join up with the tidal river. Mrs Valentine saw me looking down. 'This building used to serve as a boathouse too,' she explained. 'I expect you'd like to see?' She seemed so unsure of herself that I deemed the moment had come to try and take advantage of the situation.

'The cost of making this place habitable would be astronomical,' I said censoriously. She was struggling with another door and did not respond immediately. I went to her side and pulled at the handle. The damp had made the door swell and jam against its frame; I had to use all my strength to force it open. Some of the slimy verdigris on the metalwork brushed against my sleeve and stained it. This trifling accident caused Mrs Valentine further confusion.

'I'm so sorry,' she said. 'I should have got Wilson to clear the place up a bit before anyone came.'

I told her not to worry and led the way in the darkness down a flight of stone steps. There was a door at the bottom and this opened when two bolts were slid back to reveal a small jetty that abutted on the waterway I had seen from the window. A padlocked metal grille was suspended across the channel to stop anybody getting onto the jetty from the marsh and a large flat-bottomed rowing boat lay on its side, pulled up out of the water; it seemed unlikely that it would still be watertight. A smell of damp and decaying vegetation hung in the air – not unusual in such a place – but there was also a more prevailing and unpleasant odour. It smelt like rotting flesh. I looked around and shivered. 'Damp must be a great problem,' I pronounced.

'There's no rising damp,' said Mrs Valentine. 'The walls are all stone.' Her tone was still apologetic and she made no attempt to tell me that a place with its own boathouse and access to the sea was at a premium in the area. I made a grunting noise and tapped one of the timbers that supported the protective structure above our heads. 'Is there any land that goes with the building?' I asked.

Mrs Valentine shook her head. 'No. The marsh is public land and I want to retain the garden. I just thought I might be able to sell off the stables.' She was almost thinking out loud. 'A little more money would be so useful. It's been very hard since Edgar died.'

'What kind of sum were you thinking of?' I asked.

She looked embarrassed and I wondered if she was going to retreat behind the words scribbled on the estate agent's card: 'Price to be resolved'. Luckily she did not. She mentioned a figure that made my heart jump with excitement. It was lower than I had dared hope for and could bear no relation to the true market value of the property. My elation was short-lived – I was not dealing directly with Mrs Valentine but through the intermediary of the estate agent. I cursed myself for having proffered his card by way of introduction; I could easily have said that I had heard a house was on the market and brazened things out later. I hoped that none of this inner turmoil showed on my face as we climbed back up the stone steps. I merely catalogued a list of the features that the building did not have: electricity, drainage, sanitation. Mrs Valentine agreed with me and said that perhaps she would be prepared to adjust her price to make allowance for these deficiencies. It occurred to me at this stage that I must show some kind of interest or even willingness to purchase. It was necessary to make the good Mrs Valentine feel obligated to honour the figure she had quoted before the self-interested estate agent got to work on her.

'It's difficult,' I said. 'I am a man of limited means. Nearly every penny I have would be needed to make this habitable.'

'I don't think I could go any lower,' she said.

'The figure would have to be in the area you have quoted,' I said. 'Then by making a few sacrifices I think my resources could just stretch to making the purchase.' I turned and looked her straight in the eyes. 'Despite its dilapidated condition I would be less than honest if I did not admit that the building and its situation exert a strange charm on me.' I was taking a risk by expressing so strong a preference but I felt it important that I struck some chord in Mrs Valentine's heart. I sensed that she was a lonely woman who missed her husband and yet was attached sentimentally to the house and surroundings in which they had presumably passed many happy days. If I could show that I shared her feelings of attachment then I would be well on the way to enlisting her commitment when it came to the inevitable tussle with the grasping estate agent.

Mrs Valentine turned away from me and again I noticed the blush on her cheek. 'It can be lovely here,' she said. 'Some of my friends think I'm foolish to stay on in the house but they don't understand.'

'I think I understand,' I said, trying to inject the right note of sympathy into my voice. 'Shall we say then that I have agreed to purchase the house at not more than the first figure you quoted?' I allowed my face to cloud over. 'There is only one thing that bothers me.'

She looked worried. 'What is it?'

'I fear that your estate agent, knowing I have expressed an interest, may try and force the price up beyond the figure that we have agreed. I don't know if you have much experience of the breed but they can behave like that. I recall that once, when I sold a house, the estate agent involved tried to persuade me to accept a higher offer that came in from a third party as the contracts were being exchanged.' I paused. 'Of course, I refused.'

'Of course.' Was there, as I hoped, in that reiteration an assurance that the price would not change? I rather thought so. Naturally, my one-time experience with the estate agent had been pure invention but it seemed to have served its purpose admirably.

'Excellent,' I said, moving towards the door. 'I will approach your estate agent when you have had time to contact him. Will tomorrow be too early?'

I wondered for a moment if I was sounding too precipitate but Mrs Valentine shook her head calmly. 'No. That will be quite all right. I'll telephone him immediately.' As we moved out into the garden Mrs Valentine indicated a small door in the outside wall. 'There's a track that goes round the outside of the property. You'll probably find that the easiest means of access. The land around the doorway can be included in the sale.'

'That seems a very good idea,' I said. 'How fortunate that your magnificent elms have been spared.'

'Yes,' she said. 'My husband was very fond of trees. I'm glad they survived him.' She cleared her throat and snapped her fingers at the spaniels who had been following us lugubriously during the tour, although they had refused to make the descent to the jetty with us. 'I hope you won't think me inquisitive but are you thinking of living here permanently or keeping the house as a holiday home?'

I felt that she wanted to know more about me than was suggested by the straightforward nature of the question, but something made me reluctant to answer. 'I'm approaching retirement,' I said at length. 'My idea would be to get the house into sufficiently good condition to move into at that date. I certainly couldn't afford to own two homes.'

'Perhaps you are in the same situation as myself?' she said.

I hesitated and she blushed again, at the same time extending an arm to touch my sleeve. 'Forgive me if I mention something you would rather not talk about.'

'No, no,' I said. 'I have a wife. She is here with me now in Blanely. She has a slight chill so I left her where we are staying.' Was it my imagination or did a fleeting expression of regret pass across Mrs Valentine's face? 'I hope she will like the house,' she said simply.

'I'm certain she will,' I said. 'She's enchanted by the region.' It was strange but I found that once I started inventing the truth each successive lie came easier than the last. If necessary I could have peopled a landscape with figures, all of my own creation.

I took a respectful leave of Mrs Valentine and made my way down the drive feeling that her eyes were following me. I had applied a subtle pressure to her hand and held it just a trifle longer than was necessary. In this way I hoped she would appreciate that I was reminding her of the bargain we had made and also, perhaps, expressing an incipient warmth of feeling that would have sounded importunate if conveyed by words.

I left the gate and walked a few hundred yards till I had an uninterrupted view across the marshes. Once again the sight produced a sense of awe and suppressed fear that revealed itself as a kind of excitement. There was something menacing about the flat, windswept land draining into the sea and yet I felt myself drawn to it. Whatever destiny I had belonged here.

No sooner had this realization occurred to me than it was followed by the reality. Although I had blithely said that my wife found the area enchanting, this was the opposite of the truth – she had done nothing but complain since our arrival. Furthermore, she controlled the purse strings; it was her legacy that would be required to pay for the property. In her present mood she hardly seemed likely to feel well disposed either towards me or the semi-derelict house.

I returned to the inn wondering what to do for the best. If Mrs Valentine stuck to her word and remained unswayed by the estate agent then I would be expected to proceed with the purchase the following day. Of course, if I did nothing, then no harm would be done; Mrs Valentine might feel a pang of regret but the dwelling would soon be sold to someone else and for a better price. It all depended on my wife. I had twenty-four hours to persuade her that Marsh Cottage, as I had already decided to call it, would make an ideal purchase for our retirement. It occurred to me that I should have made an appointment with Mrs Valentine for a return visit accompanied by my wife. She would have to see the place.

When I got back to our room I found my wife in one of her worst moods. She was now dressed and complaining that she had been kept waiting for her breakfast. When I innocently commented that she should have gone down by herself as she had done for lunch the previous day, she flew into a rage and demanded what conclusions I wanted the other guests to draw from the behaviour of a wife who was forced to eat alone because her husband was never there. Was I trying to make her a figure of ridicule and contempt? Was I trying to make it clear to everybody that our marriage was a mockery?

This, though by no means an atypical beginning to a day in my married life, was not how I wanted this one to begin. I apologized fulsomely and gave assurances that I would never leave her side for the rest of our holiday together. I asked her what she would like to do and whether there was any special treat I could procure for her breakfast.

If anything, my contrition seemed to make her even more annoyed. She returned to my choice of a holiday on the Broads as a subject for further abuse and assured me that the last few days had been amongst the most miserable that she had ever spent. The sound of her voice must have been heard all over the inn and when we eventually came downstairs it was obvious from the landlord's manner that he found us far from being ideal guests. My wife complained that the tea was cold and sent back her boiled egg because it was overdone. I tried to smooth things over but it was a relief when I eventually persuaded her into the car for what I described as an 'excursion'. I felt that her mood could only improve and that the more time it was given to do so the better as far as property viewing was concerned. I would drive her around the local countryside and encourage her to eat a large lunch. This, with the aid of a few gin and limes, might induce a more sanguine humour. Though by no means an alcoholic my wife did enjoy the occasional tipple and was sometimes quite tractable afterwards.

My plan was to visit a number of local monuments which I hoped would prove interesting and might even awaken in her a flicker of enthusiasm for the area. Unfortunately, nearly all of them had closed with the end of the tourist season, and we were thus restricted to looking across moats and up at barred gatehouses. The promise of the early morning faded and a fine drizzle began to fall, pressing a pall of mist down on the landscape. Having criticized everything that she had seen and not seen, my wife fell to complaining about my driving. It was either too fast or too slow, too timid or too reckless; I was a poor judge of distance and had no powers of concentration. It was a refrain that I had heard many times before but today, perhaps because I was overwrought and worried about the house, it began to unsettle me. I overshot a turning – despite all her criticism, she expected me to map read as well as drive – and then reversed too fast, nearly colliding with a brewer's dray coming out of the side road. There was a screech of brakes, an angry blast on the horn and the back of the Morris was nearly under the driver's cabin. My wife let out an ear-piercing scream and pressed her hand against her bosom. The driver of the dray let out a few choice remarks and I quickly drove away from the scene of the incident.

'Are you mad?' she demanded. 'Have you completely taken leave of your senses?' I apologized but she continued to dramatize the incident, making melodramatic claims that I had nearly given her a heart attack. At this moment we passed a respectable looking pub and I pulled into the car park.

'You need a drink,' I said firmly.

This statement provoked no argument and we entered the saloon bar where a log fire blazed in the grate, a large red setter stretched out before it. I ordered my wife a double brandy and she sat before the fire and talked to the red setter, who rested his head upon her knee and gazed up at her with adoring and uncomprehending eyes. I felt a sudden affection for the dog because in a way that I could never have done it was putting my wife in a better humour. She had a second brandy and talked to the landlord's wife about dogs. The woman had an affected upper-class accent and my wife soon began to imitate the inflection – an imitation of an imitation. I did not think that Mrs Valentine would warm to my wife.

My wife was hardly saying a word to me but, when I suggested that we stayed where we were for lunch, she agreed and said nothing when I ordered a bottle of wine. She drank most of this and had her third double brandy before I called for the bill. She was not noticeably drunk but talking volubly and waving her arms about freely enough to knock a string of horse brasses from the wall. Her relationship with the red setter had now progressed to the point where she called him her 'lovely boy'. When I suggested that the country was the only place to have a dog she did not disagree with me. All in all, I felt that I had salvaged something from a potential disaster. Now I had to capitalize on the ground I had won.

'What would you like to do, dear?' I said as we left the pub. 'Perhaps a little nap would be nice.'

'I do feel sleepy,' she said. 'You shouldn't have made me eat that trifle.'

I said nothing but felt her settle heavily in the seat beside me. She leant back and momentarily closed her eyes before putting on her seat belt. 'And drive carefully for heaven's sake. We don't want another accident.'

'No, dear.'

I eased my foot off the clutch and took a route that I knew would bring me back to Blanely along the coast road. The rain had stopped, the mist had lifted and a feeble sun was trying to break through the light covering of cloud. The view across the marshes was unimpaired, and I saw a hawk swooping down into the reeds. 'It has a certain wild charm doesn't it?' I said.

My wife's chin was drooping forward towards her bosom, her eyelids flickered. 'What?'

'The landscape. It's like a painting isn't it?'

My wife grunted and I did not pursue the matter. She was clearly not interested and I could think of no oblique way of approaching the question of the house. I would have to come right out with it – make a bold statement of what I wanted. This would be best made on the spot; if I described the property she would probably refuse even to see it. Heart thumping, I put my foot down and immediately received a caution to drive slower. For a malicious moment I thought of the brewer's dray smashing into the car and crushing her in a tangle of twisted metal; I saw a sheet being pulled over an inert body and a white-coated figure turning to me and shaking his head. The picture was so vivid that it frightened me.

We came round a bend and the road straightened out. Two miles ahead lay Blanely and I could see the elms which marked the Valentine property. Tall trees, like church towers, were landmarks in this part of the world.

'I want to show you something,' I said to her. 'I've found something that could be a real investment.'

She had nearly drifted off again and sat up irritably. 'What are you talking about?'

'Houses around here sell for very extravagant sums,' I said. 'Just out of interest I looked at a very ordinary little bungalow in the village. Do you know how much they wanted for it?'

My wife said that she did not and I quoted a figure slightly in excess of the true one. 'You're not thinking of moving out here, are you?' she said.

I changed down to third and prepared to brake. We were almost level with Marsh House. 'I'm thinking of the money we could make. I've found something that could be worth a small fortune with a little bit spent on it.'

Just past the flint wall that marked the end of the property was a farm track that skirted the marsh. My wife's eyes widened as I pulled off the road. 'Down here?'

'The lady who owns it is prepared to sell it for a fraction of what it's worth.'

'Sell what? What are you talking about?'

'A little house,' I said. 'You'll see in a minute.'

We splashed through water-filled pot holes and my wife looked at me as if I were mad. My plan was obvious. The only way to excite her interest would be to treat the purchase as a financial enterprise that could turn her small legacy into the beginnings of a fortune.

'Lots of people scramble to find houses around here,' I said. 'They come down from the Midlands at weekends. Yachtsmen, bird watchers, golfers. It's a playground for the rich.'

We bumped round the corner of the wall that protruded furthest into the marsh and the stables lay visible ahead, the gaping hole in the collapsed roof clearly visible. My wife's expression was incredulous. 'Is that it?' she asked.

'It has its own boathouse and access to the sea,' I explained eagerly. 'Repair the roof and tidy up inside and it could be worth £40,000 – maybe more. It doesn't look much at the moment but the situation is perfect for people who like their privacy. You could never put your money to better use.' I stopped the car and she craned her head to look up at the grey flint walls. On this side, exposure to the elements had rotted the majority of the window frames and some of the panes were broken. I noticed that the door that gave access to the garden was ajar.

The expression on my wife's face was thoughtful. '£40,000, you think?'

I felt a stab of elation: she sounded interested. My plan was working. 'At least. There's no way of knowing what the right buyer would pay for this place. Come and have a look.' I got out of the car and walked round to the passenger door. I stretched out my hand to open it and found that it was locked. She was looking up at me with an expression of loathing and contempt on her face. 'You poor fool,' she sneered. 'Do you really think I'd part with my money for a dump like this? I wouldn't take it as a gift. It makes my flesh creep just to look at it.'

My hopes were cruelly dashed and I could feel the nails digging into my palms as I clenched my fists. 'Be reasonable,' I said. 'You're turning your back on a real opportunity.' I shook the door handle but she would not open it. I began to lose my temper – I think I was almost in tears. 'If you don't help me buy this place, you'll regret it!'

'Don't be so stupid, you pathetic little man,' she said. 'I'm not getting out of this car.'

I turned away and took a number of steps to the edge of the marsh. Below me was the dyke that led to the boathouse. A dead rat was suspended in the water, head up, tail down, its paws on the surface almost as if it was praying. It was covered in worms. They writhed and wriggled from every part of its body like waving tentacles; the water in the area of the rat was a dense cloud of them. I felt a wave of disgust and walked back to the car. My wife was powdering her nose.

CHAPTER THREE

When we got back to the inn my wife went straight upstairs to our room. We had not exchanged a word since driving away from Marsh House. I was depressed beyond measure but in a way that made me incapable of taking any positive action. I felt as if all my enthusiasm for life had been crushed out of me.

After about half an hour of sitting in the empty residents' lounge and listening to a wireless playing somewhere in the recesses of the inn I decided to go out. I would take a walk across the marshes to the beach – the fresh air might help blow away some of the gloom. Without giving the matter great thought, I found myself leaving the church behind and taking the path that led across the marsh to the bunker where I had sheltered from the storm. My surprise can be imagined when I heard somebody following me and turned to find my wife.

'Are you looking for another bargain?' she jeered. 'What is it this time, a lighthouse? I want to see what you get up to when you go off by yourself. The very idea of buying anything in this wilderness – you must be mad.'

I soon realized that she was in one of her vindictive moods, exacerbated by the drink. In this condition she could worry any bone to toothpicks and she had clearly pursued me purely for the pleasure of tormenting me.

'If you think you're going to get your hands on my money you've got another think coming,' she chanted. 'I'm going to keep control of every penny.' I looked ahead to what I thought was the bunker and then recognized the long grey outline of the sluice gate just visible above the waving rushes and some coils of barbed wire, no doubt left over from the war. The path narrowed so that my wife had to fall in behind me. Her voice pursued me above the sound of the wind. 'You'll be lucky if you get anything in my will. You don't deserve it – making my life a misery. Why did I ever have to marry such a stupid, wet little man? It wasn't as if everybody didn't warn me.'

I said nothing but continued along the path. I could see the dunes now, and the sluice was only thirty yards away. My heart was bumping. The voice behind me was a goad that could only be there to force me to act. Some destiny had willed that she should follow me; it was predetermined. I quickened my stride and drew ahead of my wife though not her voice.

'Are you running away?' she called after me. 'That's what you always do, isn't it? Why couldn't I have married a *man*?'

I got to the sluice and hurried to its middle. The snapped stanchion was still suspended precariously by the rusty hand rail. I felt behind me gingerly. The concrete trembled as if alive. I looked down into the water and pretended to react in horror. 'Don't come any further! ' I threw up a warning arm and turned towards my wife.

She paused at the edge of the sluice and placed her hands on her hips. 'Are you threatening me?'

'It's not that. I think there's a body down here.' My voice almost broke and perhaps it was this and the nervous falsity of my performance that persuaded my wife that I was telling the truth.

She took a step forward. 'What are you talking about?' She looked at me, wary and uncertain but unable to resist looking.

'It's horrible,' I said. I scrambled over the parapet onto one of the bastions so that I was behind the loose block of concrete. 'There's a pole here if I can reach it.' I dropped to one knee and pretended to be leaning over the water. All the time I was watching my wife. She advanced slowly, her hand gripping the rail. I rose to my feet. 'Careful,' I said. 'The rail is loose.'

She was looking down into the water. Her face had already prepared an expression of distaste; her eyes were narrowed, her lips drawn back. She stopped in front of me, with the concrete block between us. 'Where?' She leaned forward.

For what seemed like a full minute, I hesitated. I seemed to be paralysed, not with fear but with uncertainty. Did I really want to kill my wife? I knew that in these few seconds her life hung in the balance. Turned away from me and looking down into the water, she seemed unmenacing, almost vulnerable. Then she spoke.

'It's a rock, you stupid idiot!' That harsh, scathing voice acted as a trigger. I don't know whether I actually pushed or whether I merely leant forward, no longer able to control my anger. Whatever the motivation, my body collided with the block of concrete and it tilted forward. She turned her head and screamed as she saw what was happening. The block caught her above the hips and precipitated her forward. The rail parted like a straw and she disappeared from view.

Horrified, I ran to the edge. Her body was draped over a large rock which must have originally formed part of the foundation on which the sluice gate was built. Her buttocks were tilted into the air and the slab of concrete lay across the small of her back, pinning her down so that her head and shoulders were beneath the water. She was not dead. Her legs kicked and she was struggling to arch her back and draw her head from the water. She was like some half-crushed insect in its death agonies. I watched in awe and marvelled at her strength. Her will to survive was incredible. Her head rose and with a ghastly choking sound she jerked her shoulders and managed to shove the slab of concrete a few inches sideways. For a second it seemed that she was actually going to struggle free.

I do not know whether it was through compassion or instinct but I felt a sudden impulse to go to her aid. I found myself scrambling down the bank and my feet oozing into the mud. The water was freezing cold but I hardly noticed it as I waded forward. Her head rose again and blood gushed from her mouth. I paused, trying to conquer my horror. Immediately, I started to sink. I was a man trapped in a nightmare. I jerked forward again and, in my clumsy desperation, stumbled and fell across her body. My weight was now added to that of the concrete pressing her head and shoulders deeper beneath the fast-flowing water. I felt her twitch and shudder and rolled aside, crying out in my terror. Her hair streamed out beneath the water and strands brushed against my wrist. The mud swirled up so that I could see individual particles of sand dancing before her dying face like motes in a sunbeam. At that moment there was a rush of blood-flecked bubbles from her mouth and her body went limp. I knew that now she must be dead. Even without meaning to I had been the final agent of her destruction.

I staggered to my feet and waded to the bank. I was shivering and it was not only with the cold. I had killed my wife. The enormity of the act was almost beyond comprehension. I slapped my arms across my body and tried to calm myself. Whatever I did, I must not panic. I took several deep breaths and reviewed the situation. The fact that I was soaked to the skin did not alarm me as far as the police were concerned; it was logical that a distraught husband should have plunged into the stream to try and save his wife. I steeled myself to walk across the sluice gate and look down at her immobile body and the surrounding area. Satisfied that there was nothing incriminating, I hurried back to the village and blurted out to the landlord that a terrible accident had befallen my wife. Using all my recently practised acting skills, I described how my wife had gone on ahead whilst I tried to locate a wild bird in the sedge. I had thought I heard a scream but it was not until I reached the sluice gate that I discovered a block of concrete had overbalanced and crushed my wife beneath the water. At this point I broke down completely and the landlord rang for the police and the local doctor. My breakdown was by no means totally contrived. With every second that passed, the realization of what I had done became more acute. It was ironic but in my sense of isolation and loneliness I found myself looking around for my wife, the very person I had murdered.

I knew that I would never hear her voice again, touch her,

climb into the same bed as her – that whole areas of space she had occupied around me would now be empty. I had wanted to be rid of her but now she was gone I was not so sure. Above all, I was confused and I knew that in confusion lay danger, a danger of blurting out the truth. I drank sparingly of the brandy that I was given and excused myself by saying I had a weak stomach for spirits, but in reality I was frightened of taking anything that might loosen my tongue. I changed into the clothes that had only recently been dried from my soaking on the beach and waited for the arrival of the doctor and the police.

Doctor Parr was a local man, elderly and taciturn. He insisted on giving me a sedative and clearly found it difficult to find any topic of conversation that fitted the situation. I imagined that he probably had a coterie of ancient patients whom he treated like cattle. The panda car took longer to come because it had been called to an accident and I heard the young sergeant saying that it had been 'one of those days'. He blushed when he realized that I might have overheard him.

Some of the locals had gone on ahead and when we got to the sluice there were already half a dozen people there, amongst whom I recognized the man who had been digging for worms on the beach. I thought he gave me a strange, knowing glance but decided that I must not let my imagination start exaggerating things; if he had seen me before it was of no importance. A fire had been lit on the bank and this provided light as well as warmth, for it was now getting dark.

'She's dead all right,' I heard somebody mutter to the sergeant. 'Slab of concrete must have crushed the life out of her. Doubt if she felt a thing.'

Little do you know, I thought to myself. I hung back from the water's edge and followed the sergeant's suggestion that I should go and stand by the fire. One of the other men who stood there was rubbing his hands together above the flames and he nodded awkwardly as I came up, unable to look me in the eye. I noticed that everybody appeared uncomfortable in my presence. Was this in its strained way an expression of sympathy or did it perhaps indicate that I was under suspicion? That at the back of everybody's mind was a query as to whether I had been responsible for my wife's death? Again, I told myself not to start imagining things. Nobody but an onlooker could prove that my wife's death was not an accident. On an impulse I turned towards the man who had been digging worms on the beach. He was looking at me, and I turned away again quickly. That knowing glance he had given me on my arrival: did it signify anything? Despite the cold, I felt myself beginning to sweat. My heart was pounding. I felt that the men standing near me must hear it and draw their own conclusions – but at the same time I knew that I must stay calm. This was only the beginning.

There was a slapping noise and I saw the doctor pulling on a pair of fisherman's waders. It was quite dark now and a mist was coming in off the sea. In the background the dunes looked like a row of mountains silhouetted against the night sky. The wind rustled through the reed beds. I think I would have been frightened even without the knowledge that the woman I had murdered was lying in the water just a few yards away. But as I was frightened I was also exhilarated. The electric feeling of tension and fear of imminent discovery boosted all my senses. It was like a drug. I felt a strange sense of identity with my surroundings – the whispering reeds, the dancing grasses on the dunes – they had conspired with me, they knew my secret. Though I did not trust them I felt with them, I shared their wild free spirit.

The sergeant held a flashlight and waded into the river with the doctor. Other men moved forward, no doubt motivated as much by morbid curiosity as by any desire to help, and more lights played upon the scene. I too moved forward. I suddenly felt a desire not to remain by myself and I wanted to read the messages on the men's faces. If there was a hint of suspicion, an exchange of knowing glances, I wanted to profit by it. With a shock of recognition I saw my wife virtually as I had left her but now completely submerged by the incoming tide. The torches shone through the water and her head moved slightly from side to side as though she were still alive and struggling feebly to free herself. The sight made me feel sick. Her long hair had escaped from the coil in which she pinned it, and was snaking down her back; her body had started to form an obstacle which trapped scraps of reed and driftwood carried by the tide. Already she seemed to have changed so much that I hardly recognized her. In the torchlight her flesh looked chalk white, and I could see that her skirt had billowed out in the water to expose her thighs.

The sergeant took off his watch and he and Doctor Parr reached beneath the water and attempted to move the concrete slab. I was relieved to see that they did not find it easy. That my wife could have budged it at all seemed a miracle and paid witness to the strength imparted by the human will to survive. Sand and mud were stirred up as the men struggled and it needed somebody to help the doctor before the slab was eased to one side. My wife's body rose up through the cloudy water as if under levitation and I experienced another pang of fear and foreboding. I found it difficult to believe that she was really dead – at every instant I expected her to rise to her feet and point an accusing finger at me. Every listless movement that she made in the water hinted to me of the existence of life. I was nervous and I hoped that it did not reveal itself as guilt.

The doctor passed his hands quickly over my wife's back and, after a brief interchange with the sergeant that I could not catch, stood up. The sergeant slid his hands beneath the corpse and lifted. There was a release of breath from those around me and somebody patted my arm sympathetically. I nodded and watched him deposit the sodden, dripping burden with the head hanging down, the matted hair and fragments of floating matter obscuring the face. Seeing that heavy parcel of flesh there was no doubt left in my mind: she was dead. I felt a little easier. No photographs had been taken to pinpoint the position of my wife's body; everybody was proceeding as if they accepted that her death had been an accident. I saw Doctor Parr looking at me and promptly turned away, covering my face with my hands. Within seconds the young constable who had accompanied the sergeant was at my side.

'Beg pardon, sir, but I'm afraid there's the formality of identification.' His tone was apologetic to the point of being abject. I rubbed my hand across my mouth and followed. The onlookers stepped respectfully aside. I thought to myself, this will be the last time that I have to look at her. After this she will be put in a box and I will say that to look upon her again would be too distressing for me. The thought gave me the courage that I needed. One last look.

My wife had been laid near the fire, and Doctor Parr was kneeling beside her. The sergeant came towards me. 'I'm sorry,' he said. 'I know this must be very distressing for you.'

I said nothing but approached my wife. There was sufficient light from the fire but the constable shone a torch. She lay on her back with her face towards the sky, a pall of hair obscuring her features. The doctor pulled it aside like a curtain and I sucked in breath sharply. Her eyes were like pigeon eggs, the irises barely visible beneath the lids. Her cheeks were grotesquely swollen. For a moment I wondered if it really was her. 'Yes,' I whispered.

At that instant, the head flopped sideways towards me and the mouth opened uttering a low groan. There was no doubt some straightforward anatomical reason for this – the release of pent up air trapped in some cavity of the body – but I started back in terror. There was in the sound a chilling note of reproach and despair that made my flesh creep. I stood trembling and as I looked down saw something appear at the corner of the pouting mouth. It was a worm. Thin, red, and no more than two inches long, its loathsome body spilled over the dead lips and dropped to the ground. Rearing its head as if seeking which direction to take, it stabbed at the air and began to loop towards me fast. The head of a second worm appeared from my wife's nostril. Unable to control myself, I cried out and stepped back. My foot trod on the fire and a cloud of sparks blew across my wife's corpse, turning into black specks against her eyeballs. I fainted.

CHAPTER FOUR

Almost six months to the day after my wife was cremated I came to live at Marsh Cottage. It had not been an easy time and when I first stood in the large downstairs room of the completed house and looked across the marsh I felt as if I had returned from a long journey.

An official examination of the sluice had shown that owing to erosion caused by the forces of nature – spring tides, storms and floods – the whole structure of the sluice gate, which had been constructed hurriedly during the war at the same time as the blockhouse, was in danger of collapse. The concrete blocks could have tumbled at any time, it was said. My unfortunate wife had perished by the million-to-one chance that decreed that she should be passing when the first one fell. The sluice gate was dismantled and rebuilt and others in the neighbourhood examined and fortified; there was even talk of an action for damages against the Ministry of Defence but nothing came of this. The coroner was sympathetic and the inquest a formality.

The funeral service and cremation were more arduous, but fortunately neither my wife nor I had accumulated many relations and only a few of those attended the last rites which were held in Romford. The legal arrangements were more complex. If any lingering suspicion existed about the manner of my wife's death, I did not wish to inflame them by pressing for a speedy probate of her will. I had to let the law take its course which it did at a pace sufficiently slow as to make sight or sound of the word solicitor anathema to me. All the time that I was waiting for the will to be read, I remembered my wife's mocking words when she followed me across the marsh, her statement that I would never get my hands on her inheritance. Was it possible that she had actually changed her will without telling me? I knew that she had made one because we had both done so in the early days of our marriage, leaving everything to each other. I thought that there was a copy of her will at the bank but I made no inquiries about it for fear of raising suspicions. Better to wait and worry.

Eventually I received a letter suggesting a date for me to call at the solicitor's office. It was above a furniture shop, I recall, up a dark flight of stairs between scuffed walls. I heard the sound of a typewriter and went into an outer office where a girl typed between piled in-trays. A middle-aged man and a youth looked at me curiously as if they knew who I was and wanted to read every detail that my face had to offer. I was shown into a very small room and vaguely recognized the face of the man behind the desk. He had handled the purchase of our flat – or rather *my* flat. He made no effort to shake hands but gestured to a chair and began what I imagined must be a prepared speech about how he sympathized with my loss and apologized for the delay in 'sorting things out'. This was apparently due to tardiness on the part of others.

I half listened to him and raised my eyes to the wall behind his chair where a painting hung in a heavy black frame. It was a strange painting to find in a solicitor's office, being in the manner of Hieronymus Bosch, the fifteenth-century Dutch mystic. It might even have been a reproduction of one of his own paintings for all I know. The subject was clearly hell because devils with grotesque sharp-featured faces and forked tails were engaged in the torture and humiliation of creatures part animal and part human. Flames rose about the twisted, mis-shapen monsters that were being crushed, broken on racks or torn apart with giant pincers. It was a terrifying scene, yet at the same time almost hypnotic in its ability to draw and absorb the eye. One detail in particular caught my attention – a figure lying in the forefront of the painting. Something about its position immediately reminded me of my wife when she was lying near the sluice gate. The slightly bloated body, the tilt of the head, the blank-eyed expression of despair, the half-open mouth . . . I controlled a shiver and returned my gaze to the solicitor, who was untying a piece of string around a buff folder. 'As you are probably aware, your wife benefited from a will made by her spinster aunt.'

I nodded. 'Poor woman,' I said. 'She never had a chance to reap any pleasure from it.' I watched his face carefully in case his expression told me otherwise.

'This of course forms part of her estate which she leaves entirely to you. There are no other bequests.'

'Oh.' I hoped that the exclamation did not betray the relief that I felt. I caught the solicitor's probing eye and turned away. Against my will I found myself looking at the painting again. In some subtle way, it seemed to have changed. There was now something emerging from the mouth of the figure in the foreground. It trailed down like a piece of curling string.

'Are you all right?' I did not reply to the solicitor's question but continued to stare at the painting. He turned round. 'Awful thing, isn't it? A legacy from my predecessor. I keep meaning to take it down and find something more cheerful.' He turned back to his file and produced a pair of horn-rimmed spectacles from a leather case. It must be my imagination but now another black, waving line had sprouted from the corpse . . . And another. I felt as if a cold hand had been placed on my shoulder, and a shiver ran down my spine – I must be seeing things, I was experiencing some kind of nervous breakdown. I rose to my feet.

'I'd like a glass of water, please,' I said, my voice hoarse.

'Of course, of course.' The solicitor rose to his feet. 'Are you sure you're all right? You've gone as white as a sheet.'

'I'm sorry,' I said. 'I was thinking about my wife. All this brings it back.'

'I quite understand.' He went to the door and called for a glass of water.

When he came back I was sitting in a chair with my back to

the painting. The last time that I had looked at it, the corpse had been covered in worms rising into the air like sprouting seeds. I was convinced I was going mad, especially since this was not the first time that my imagination had started playing tricks. I was living a series of waking nightmares, all of them having one thing in common. The worms seemed to be everywhere – in my thoughts and in my life – and more and more bringing my wife back to me. There was no escape from her; it was as if I had been placed in the same coffin with her and forced to watch the process of putrefaction. But she had been cremated; the coffin had been burnt, and I deliberately reminded myself of the moment when it rolled into the furnace and the panel slid shut. Suddenly I remembered the effigies in Blanely church and the design on the side of the tombs, the worms reaching up like flames – 'the worms of hell' the vicar had called them. It was a frightening recollection, as if everything had been preordained and I was a pawn in some strange manifestation of the supernatural. I had set out to free myself and yet I seemed trapped.

My hand brushed against the proffered glass of water and then guided it shakily to my lips. The solicitor's voice seemed to come from a long way away. 'You must start leading your own life now,' he said calmly. 'I'm certain your wife would have wanted it that way.'

The most difficult thing, of course, had been to preserve a hold on Marsh Cottage – the proposed name had become a reality in my mind. After the death of my wife I could hardly have arrived on Mrs Valentine's doorstep breathless with news of the impending purchase. However, if I had done nothing she would surely have thought that my wife's death had ruled out all possibility of a sale. I therefore had to find some means of preserving my interest and her obligation without behaving in a suspicious fashion. At first I thought of telephoning her and then I decided that a personal approach would be much more effective. My short acquaintance with Mrs Valentine had persuaded me that she would be more easily manoeuvred when face to face with me rather than talking over the phone.

In the end I rang her up and then went to see her just before leaving for London. Word of mouth had quickly brought her news of what had happened, and she blurted out some conventional condolences, then readily agreed when I asked if I might call on her.

It was a grey overcast day, I recall, and the bushes were still glistening from a recent shower as I drove up to the house. It suddenly loomed out of the shrubbery and a man who was trimming the grass verges looked towards me. With a start I realized that it was the man who had been digging for worms on the beach, the one who had looked on when my wife's body was recovered. He was about fifty, with a weather-beaten face and a malign, insolent expression. I remembered Mrs Valentine saying that she had a man in a couple of hours each week and assumed that it was him. He turned back to his work and I stopped the car outside the main house. Mrs Valentine quickly appeared at the doorway and I noticed she was wearing a grey silk dress with a wool cardigan and double row of pearls. Her hair freshly done.

'Poor Mr Hildebrand,' she exclaimed as I stepped from the car. 'I can't tell you how shocked I was when I heard the terrible news. You have all my sympathy.'

'Thank you, Mrs Valentine,' I said. 'I have no wish to trespass on too much of your time. There is just one thing that I wanted to say to you—'

She held up a restraining hand. "You don't have to say anything,' she assured me. 'I quite understand. Obviously this accident has changed all your plans for the future. You need feel no obligation to proceed with our agreement.'

'On the contrary,' I said. 'I want to explain to you that what has happened has not changed my desire to live here – quite the reverse. In this way I will always be near my poor wife. It was so ironic that feeling about the area as she did she should have perished in that way.'

Mrs Valentine involuntarily extended both her hands and grasped mine. 'I know your feelings exactly,' she said. 'It is the memory of a loved one that binds me to this place. I congratulate you for so quickly coming to terms with your true sentiments. I was so confused after my husband's death.' I wondered for an instant if there was some oblique criticism in her words but a glance into her wide, unflinching eyes told me that they were spoken without malice. 'Have you perhaps got time for a cup of tea before your journey?'

'You are very kind,' I said. 'I just hope you understand that I will be unable to put plans in motion for the immediate purchase of the building. I will be completely absorbed with all the matters pertaining to my wife's death.'

'Of course,' she said. 'Your refinement of spirit does you credit. I have already spoken to the estate agent and made him aware of my wishes.' Her face clouded. 'You were right in thinking that he would have an opinion to express upon the matter.' I spread my arms wide preparatory to speaking but no words were necessary: she touched me gently on the arm and stepped to one side. 'But all that is over. Now, please join me in a cup of tea.' She turned towards the lawn. 'You are aware of the time, Wilson?'

'Yes, ma'am. I'll just finish this border.' The lawn trimmers started to clip again and the sound reminded me that they had remained silent during my exchange of words with Mrs Valentine. Wilson had presumably been listening to every word that passed between us. His eyes caught mine and again I had the impression of a knowing glance and a slight shake of the head; his expression said 'You're a sly one and no mistake.' I thought back to the argument with my wife when I had brought her to see the house and she refused to get out of the car. The side gate to the house had been open and now that I recalled it there had been a compost heap against the wall; was it possible that Wilson had been working in the garden on that day and heard what had passed between me and my wife? My blood ran cold. He would be aware that my wife was no lover of the region and that the sentiments she had expressed cast a questionable light on the declaration I had just made to Mrs Valentine. I felt uneasy as I passed through the doorway into the tall, dark hall. Wilson would be a man who needed careful watching.

So many books and articles have been written on the problems of restoring old buildings that I feel I may forgo a long description here. Suffice it to say that it was not easy to find a local builder prepared to take on the job and, when I eventually found one, it was even more difficult to make him stick at it. Time and money ebbed away and there were occasions when I feared that the repairs would never be finished. Of course, during the majority of the time I was working in London and I had to rely on telephone calls to the builders and Mrs Valentine to tell me what was happening. Often the reports would be quite different from each other and I knew that Mrs Valentine was acting as a kind of genteel on-site foreman, cajoling and hectoring on my behalf.

The day fixed for my retirement arrived and the house was still not ready. The electrical work had not been completed, nor had the water been connected. Matters were further complicated by the fact that I had sold my flat and the new owners had stipulated that they should move in on a date that coincided with my retirement. There seemed to be nothing for it but to camp in the unfinished house. It might be a blessing in disguise as I was convinced that I would be better able to control the builders if I was on the spot.

One duty remained before the closure of what I had come to consider as my 'old' life: my actual retirement from the quantity surveyor's office where I had worked for almost thirty years. It may seem strange but in the course of that time I had never become particularly close friends with anybody on the staff, nor had I derived a great deal of satisfaction from my work; such promotion as I had known had merely been a case of stepping into dead men's shoes. When I heard that there was going to be a presentation I was almost annoyed;

such occasions are usually an embarrassment to all concerned and I knew that in my case it would be even more of a formality than most. The thought of the gift that I would receive exercised a little of my curiosity and I hoped that it would be something useful rather than decorative.

In the event I was surprised to receive a set of encyclopedias. Apparently, so the managing director informed me, I had earned the reputation of someone whose opinion was always sought when there was an argument to be settled in the office, and he told the small group of us, awkwardly clutching sherry glasses, that in my retirement I would now have the time and the means to become even better informed. I muttered the obligatory word of thanks and a insincere invitation to my old colleagues to come and see me whenever – unlikely event – they were passing my new abode and thankfully took my leave wishing, I must confess, that I had been given a less cumbersome present. I did not even bother to open the encyclopedias.

A telephone call had alerted Mrs Valentine to my arrival and I travelled down in the Morris, leading the removal van that was carrying the items of furniture I had decided to salvage from the flat. I would have preferred to abandon all of it and start afresh, but with my limited means this was not possible. My wife and I had long ago decided to sleep in separate beds, so I sold hers. Other objects which bore the stamp of her personality were also taken to the auctioneers' saleroom, including a dressing-table before which she had spent hours sighing at her reflection and brushing her hair. She had been proud of her hair, sometimes combing it over her shoulders before going to bed, at other times braiding it into long serpentine pigtails which she would then coil onto her head. With the dressing-table went the armchair that she always sat in, and her favourite painting which hung facing the front door of the flat. It depicted wild white stallions galloping through a shallow sea with a violet sunset in the background. Quite what chord it struck in my wife I never truly understood – no doubt it satisfied some secret escapist desire that she hardly dared confess even to herself. I found the stallions with their overemphasized manes and tails, snorting nostrils and threshing hooves vulgar in the extreme. Not to see them posturing before me every time I came home would be an indescribable relief. An ugly cake stand of which she was very proud, a small table on which I was never allowed to place anything in case it scratched the French polish, and a high-backed Victorian chair that she was continually telling me was Chippendale: they all went.

Of course, there was hardly any money to be made out of these sales but I wanted as far as possible to separate myself from anything that forcibly reminded me of my wife's suffocating and over-riding presence. In that case, you may ask, why go and live in the locale where I had murdered her? Because with that act I associated freedom and not repression. Because Blanely was where I had liberated myself after thirty years of a marriage too quickly made and too frequently repented. Also, and most important, because this lonely marshland region called to me in a way that I will never be able to describe adequately. Like an alcoholic drawn to the bottle I found myself attracted by the very thought of those desolate wastes sweeping down to the dunes and the sea, the ceaseless wind and its counterpoint melody with the sea, the ever-changing snowy mountains in the sky, the stark loneliness that struck a chord with my own spirit. It was this that had set me free – and almost at a stroke. It was like suddenly falling in love or finding that one possessed a musical skill. Because it had happened so quickly it was all the more overwhelming, exciting and – ultimately – terrifying.

I had intended to lead the van round the road that skirted Marsh House but it had been raining for several days and the driver was frightened of getting his vehicle bogged down, so I went ahead to warn Mrs Valentine whilst he manoeuvred through the overhanging trees at the entrance to the drive. I found her weeding one of the paths, a trowel in her hands and a wooden trug nearby. She brushed some wisps of hair from her eyes and seemed slightly disconcerted to see me. I think, like most women, she would have liked to have tidied herself up before my arrival.

'I didn't expect you to arrive so soon,' she said. 'With all this rain we've been having I rush out into the garden the minute it stops. The weeds are springing up everywhere but you can't set foot in the flowerbeds.'

'Where's Wilson?' I asked. 'Isn't this one of the days he comes?'

'He's ill,' she said. 'Something on his chest. It's been dragging on for some time.' She took off her gardening gloves and laid them in the trug. 'It's funny but when I went to see him the other day he asked to speak to you.'

I felt an immediate sense of unease. 'Do you know what about?'

'No, not really. He seems rather confused.' She looked embarrassed. 'He mentioned your wife for some reason. Perhaps it would be best if you did not see him.'

I reflected quickly. 'No,' I said. 'He probably wanted to offer his condolences. I think I should visit him. It seems the charitable thing to do. After all, he will be one of my new neighbours.'

I was pleased to note an approving gleam in Mrs Valentine's eye. 'It's a pleasure to hear you speak like that,' she said. 'When you read the papers and look at the television these days it's difficult to believe that there's any charity left in the world.' I nodded modestly and expressed the hope that it would not be too much of an imposition if the van with my furniture entered by the drive. My new neighbour assured me that it would not and the process of unloading my meagre belongings began.

I had looked forward to this moment of installation but, as is so often the case, the reality proved rather less than the expectation. It started to rain again just as the doors of the van were opened and the ground was soft which meant that mud was trampled into the house. The interior was cold, despite the fact that it was May, and of course there was neither running water nor electricity. Above all there was my nagging fear concerning Wilson. I could not help but feel that he knew something; I would not be able to rest until I had seen him.

Within the hour my furniture and belongings were unloaded and I sat on the edge of a tea chest and glumly considered the task of stowing everything away that now faced me. I heard the van disappearing down the drive and then listened to the silence. Now I was alone. It was a sobering moment; I felt like a castaway who finds himself standing on the shore of an unknown island. This was where my new life began.

I noticed that a fire had been laid in the newly finished grate and as I bent to light it there was a gentle tap on the front door. It was Mrs Valentine bearing a pot of tea.

'Oh good,' she said. 'I'm glad you found the fire. I hope you don't mind, I took the liberty of asking Betty to lay it. It's cold for the time of year, isn't it? I expect you'd care for a cup of tea after your long trip.' I accepted gratefully and listened whilst she told me about her cleaning woman, Betty, who she thought would be prepared to come in a couple of mornings a week for me if I so desired.

Mrs Valentine was going to be a very good neighbour, I decided: helpful but never overweeningly intrusive. She offered me the loan of a small cooking stove and told me where there was a tap in the garden from which I could get water but never suggested that I should use the amenities of her own house. That would clearly be overfamiliar behaviour as far as she was concerned, and I understood this attitude and respected it. Thoughtful as she was I did not wish to live cheek by jowl with her. Our cups of tea finished, she rose to take her leave and I asked her where Wilson lived.

'Surely you're not going to see him tonight? Not after your long journey and all the unpacking you have to do?'

'I may feel like a walk later on,' I said. 'I imagine he doesn't live too far away?'

Mrs Valentine assured me that he did not and described a small cottage at the end of a path on the outskirts of the village. I remember feeling relieved that it seemed a lonely spot.

'I suppose he has someone to look after him?' I asked casually.

She shook her head. 'He used to have a wife but that was some years ago. There was a scandal and she went off to live with a man in Wells. He's on his own now, as far as I know.' She smiled demurely. 'Sometimes around here, Mr Hildebrand, local people of a certain age who are alone form attachments that are not sanctified in church. You can never be certain.' She looked round the room. 'I see you have a lamp. If there is anything else you need, don't hesitate to come to the house and ask. I am usually in bed by ten though, so I would be grateful if you could call before then.'

I thanked her and saw her on her way. It was now after five o'clock and the rain was falling steadily. I unpacked for about an hour and then became bored; arranging plates and knives and forks in an unfinished kitchen was a tedious business and I suspected that it might be better to leave everything in the tea chests until all the work had been completed. I tended the fire and decided to go down and have a look at the boathouse. If the tide was in I might be able to test whether the rowing boat was seaworthy. I took the key for the water gate that I had been given by Mrs Valentine and descended the dark stairs. The door still jammed at the top and I made a note to tell the carpenter to plane a layer off the sides.

When I came out on the jetty it was to find that the tide was in – also, that there was the same disagreeable rotting smell as on my first visit. This surprised me as I had thought it must have come from the exposed muddy banks of the dyke and would disappear at high tide. I screwed up my nostrils and approached the rowing boat which was now half-propped against the back end of the jetty. The smell grew more intense. At first I thought that it must be something in the boat but there was nothing obviously visible. I pulled the boat away from the wall and immediately started back in disgust, almost letting go of the gunwale. A strip of fisherman's netting hung across the end of the dyke and entangled in it was a large dead seabird. It was a goose of some description but so clogged with oil as to make identification impossible. I imagined that the poor brute, half blinded and unable to fly, had struggled inland from the sea and eventually expired here at the end of one of the labyrinth of dykes that led off the main river. Two more pathetic bags of oily feathers suspended nearby suggested that other birds had met the same fate.

I struggled to overcome my repugnance and looked round for something to remove the grisly relics. A boat-hook hung nearby and I gritted my teeth and plucked it down. Gingerly I prodded at the large bulk of the bird and immediately, like spines on a porcupine's back, a host of red worms sprang menacingly from the blackened plumage. Their heads waved in the air as if demonstrating rage at being disturbed and one actually detached itself from the corpse it was devouring and started to crawl up the boathook towards me. Disgusted and nauseated, I hurled the staff across the jetty. Having successfully driven off my attack, the worms withdrew into the body of the bird. The stench was even more penetrating. I imagined those ghastly creatures churning through its tripes and nearly vomited. I was powerless and translated the contempt I felt for my own inability to grapple with the situation into hatred of the worms. I must destroy them, yet I could not bring myself to touch the bird again.

Thinking quickly, I remembered the paraffin that I had brought for my two lamps. I retired up the stairs and returned with the bright red can and a kitchen chair. I carefully placed the chair at the edge of the jetty against the wall and climbed onto it with the can. Conquering mounting nausea, I leaned forward and doused the three birds with paraffin. My teeth grinding together with hatred, I contemplated the fate of the worms; so far in all our encounters I had remained passive, I had not wanted to believe that I was over-reacting to coincidence. Now I felt threatened, just as I did by Wilson. It was chilling how the worms insinuated themselves into my human predicaments. As I dealt with them so must I deal with life. I splashed paraffin across the net and stepped down from the chair; as I moved it aside and screwed the cap on the can, I saw that worms were beginning to leave the bird and drop into the water. No doubt it was the paraffin driving them out, but I had an uneasy feeling that their action denoted a prescience far beyond that possessed by ordinary invertebrates. I fumbled for my matches and in my hurry spilled half the box across the floor. I struck one and tossed the flaring flame towards the netting. There was a flash and I ducked away, raising my hand to protect my face. When I turned back the dead bird was burning with a green flame and making a hissing noise like a wet log on a fire. The strands of the netting flared up and then turned black and grey. Burning worms fell writhing into the water and then sank like lead shot; there was a repetitive popping noise like a burnt sausage exploding in a frying pan. The central section of the netting parted and the feathered corpses dropped into the water; for a moment they sizzled on the surface and then slowly sank from sight, leaving a greasy film on the surface of the water.

I watched the macabre spectacle with my eyelashes singeing and the flames burning my cheeks. When I bent to pick up the boathook I found that I was breathing heavily and that my hands were shaking. I looked carefully for that worm that had been advancing towards me but it had disappeared. The wary gesture reflected my feeling towards the worms: I was frightened of them and I believed that they meant to harm me. I pulled down the rest of the netting and burnt it on the jetty, brushing the grey ash into the water. What terrified me most of all was that I associated the worms with my wife – it was as if they were her agents sent to punish me. I remembered the incident when her body had been retrieved from the sluice, the memory of the worms wriggling from her mouth and nose so powerful that it seemed to be happening all over again.

Even when I closed my eyes I could not shut it out. I turned away and something wet and slimy brushed against my cheek. I leapt backwards and found that it was a piece of fibre trailing from a folding chair that had been laid along the roof beams.

My heart was pumping and I no longer had a desire to test the rowing boat. The very thought of floating above those writhing predators in a vessel that might not be seaworthy made my flesh creep. I could imagine sinking in the water and feeling them attaching themselves to my skin. Individually at first, then in their tens, and their hundreds, and their thousands. . . .

I almost ran to the door at the foot of the stairs and closed and bolted it behind me. As I climbed I realized with a sickening sense of fear that I was already on the defensive.

I had laid out tins of sausages, beans and pineapple chunks for my supper, but now my appetite had disappeared and I put them to one side. I had never been a drinking man but I helped myself to a large measure of brandy. Once again I repeated the refrain that had been running through my mind like the burden of a popular song: 'There is nothing to fear except fear itself'. I must not get things out of proportion; the worms were unpleasant, even revolting, but they could cause me no physical harm; they were not blood-sucking leeches from the trees in some tropical jungle. It must be my worry about Wilson that was causing me to over-react. He was the danger, not a few wriggling creatures. I tried to prime myself against worries that had no rational basis and decided that I would visit Wilson as soon as it got dark. Once I had put my fears at rest there, the rest of my life might fall into place.

It was with another shot of brandy under my belt that I eventually set off towards the village. I used the side door in the wall of Marsh House and skirted the grounds. My car was parked in the driveway outside the house and I did not want to disturb Mrs Valentine – that was one of my reasons anyway. I stepped into the hedge when any cars approached and had soon covered the distance to the outskirts of the village. There was a new moon above, hardly visible through heavy cloud, and a steady drizzle to keep most people indoors. I met no one.

Mrs Valentine's directions had been precise and I had no difficulty in finding the pathway. What came as an unpleasant surprise to me was to see a police car parked beside it. There was a small hidden lay-by and I imagined that the police were operating a speed trap as people came out of the village – either that or enjoying a cigarette whilst on patrol. I waited in the shadows and it was not until a car went past that I saw by the light of its headlights that there was no one in the police car. Immediately I began to feel uneasy. Was it possible that the police were with Wilson in his cottage? Could he be making a statement? The inference may seem far-fetched but it is amazing how the mind of a guilty man will jump to conclusions when he feels threatened.

I waited for another five minutes and then heard someone coming from the direction of the path; I moved closer to the hedge until the wet foliage was brushing against my cheek and saw a policeman in a peaked cap approach the car and get into it. The light remained on and I could see that he was writing something, probably making a report. He returned a pen to his breast pocket, the light went off and seconds later the car pulled away. I waited until its lights had disappeared and debated what to do. If anything, I was even more uneasy. An owl hooted nearby and when I saw something glistening on my foot I discovered that it was a large slug. I scraped it off and stamped on it. For a reason that I could not properly analyse, I felt like turning back. The presence of the police car seemed like a warning omen. With a start of fear I wondered if the policeman was now on his way to see me ... Of course not. Nobody would know that I had arrived in the village – unless Mrs Valentine had said anything. The police were often very well informed; they knew what was going on.

In the end I decided that I would at least find out where exactly Wilson's cottage was; the policeman may well have been calling on somebody else. I approached the path and started to pick my way through the puddles. What a spring – nobody could remember one like it; the countryside was drowning, and the cottage when I came to it seemed to have sunk into the muddy ground. It was surrounded by a well-worked vegetable garden and a high hedge. It needed re-thatching and the roof had a scruffy, unkempt appearance like a pudding-basin hair-cut made with a pair of blunt scissors. The only light visible showed through a crack in the tightly drawn curtains of the room on the right of the front door.

I was wondering what to do when I heard somebody coming from the direction of the road. There was the wheezing note of an old bicycle and a light that wavered from side to side as the rider tried to steer a passage through the puddles. I panicked and ran on down the path until I found a place where I could duck in beside an overhanging tree. I did not want anyone to see me if it could be avoided. Once again I pressed back into the dripping leaves and felt icy water running down my neck. Cold and uncomfortable I waited for the cyclist to pass. Seconds turned into a minute and I realized that the bicycle must have stopped at the cottage. I peered out cautiously and retraced my footsteps. Through the hedge I could see a light bobbing towards the front door; a woman's bike had been left outside the gate. It was difficult to see clearly but I could make out the outline of a woman wearing a scarf over her head; her figure was not that of a young girl. As she approached the front door it opened and I could see Wilson silhouetted in the porch light. He reached out a hand towards the woman and she took it and allowed herself to be drawn into the cottage. At the last moment she looked back over her shoulder as if wanting to make sure that she had not been followed, and I glimpsed the face of a middle-aged woman whom I did not recognize. The door closed and all was darkness and falling rain.

Any regret that I felt about not being able to talk to Wilson was tempered with relief. At least I had avoided bumping into the police or the woman, whom I supposed to be his mistress.

Mrs Valentine had hinted at the existence of such a person in the general sense but I imagined that she was probably being discreet and had a much more exact knowledge of Wilson's domestic arrangements than she thought it politic to reveal to me. I wondered if the woman was a permanent fixture, but there had been something furtive about her arrival that suggested otherwise.

I retraced my steps down the path and walked back to Marsh House without incident. The rain was now coming down even more heavily and I decided to approach my new home by the main drive rather than via the waterlogged track that skirted the marsh. Mrs Valentine would hardly think it an intrusion at this time of night and anyway it was well past her bedtime. I approached the house down the line of glistening, dripping laurels that seemed to be choking the drive and was surprised to see that there was a light still on in one of the downstairs rooms. The impression I had formed of Mrs Valentine was that of a woman who would scrupulously turn off all lights before retiring to bed. I passed the window and then hesitated; in the few times that I had come up to Norfolk to supervise the work of the builders, I had hardly set foot inside Marsh House – I had always felt that Mrs Valentine wished to maintain a discreet distance between us and that to make a point of preserving her house as her own private domain was a sensible way of doing so. Nevertheless I was intrigued to see what lay beyond the long, dark entrance hall with its potted plants on the inlaid tables and the antelope heads staring glassy-eyed from their wooden plaques. Perhaps also I had derived a vicarious pleasure from spying on the malingering Wilson and wished to repeat the experience.

I stood still for a moment and listened. There was only the sound of the wind, and the rain pattering against the leaves. I stepped forward to the flowerbed and ducked down below the level of the window. It was wet under foot but I was already soaked after my experiences of the evening. Slowly, I raised my head, keeping to the left of the narrow opening in the curtain; I edged along the windowsill until I could see into the room. It was lofty and scattered with pieces of furniture in the grand manner; there were paintings on the wall and a fine fireplace of dark green marble. There was no fire in the grate but before it stood Mrs Valentine, wearing a long nightdress and gown of the same flimsy coffee-coloured material. She was looking up at a portrait which hung above the fireplace and showed a distinguished-looking man in a city suit. He sported a military moustache and the artist had captured the autocratic mien of a man used to giving orders. For almost a minute, Mrs Valentine stared at the portrait and I assumed that it must be of her late husband. She then turned away and skirted a long sofa to approach the table behind it, so that she was now facing me. With her hair in disarray her face seemed much softer and younger; her expression was difficult to read – calm but thoughtful, as if reflecting upon some event that lay in the past or perhaps even in the future.

On the table was a tray and from it Mrs Valentine took what at first glance I thought was a knife, then I recognized an ivory letter opener. She carried it with her and went out of the room, switching off the light behind her. She did not close the door and as she moved away towards the foot of the stairs I could see the silhouette of her naked body beneath the translucent gowns.

I hesitated, then turned back towards my house.

CHAPTER FIVE

My nocturnal rambling had prompted a number of questions but I forgot about these as I thought of my experience on the jetty and the fear returned. Now it was dark and I only had the light of two paraffin lamps to see me through the night. The dull glow from one of them illuminated an uncurtained window. I inserted the key in the lock and paused; I had a sudden horror of what I might see when I opened the door. Something caught my eye on the glistening paving stone beneath my feet: it was a long black slug. I stamped on it savagely and flung open the door. The dark shapes of the packing cases littered the room and I shone my torch amongst them as if stabbing with a sword. My teeth were clenched and my heart was pounding. Nothing seemed to have changed. I walked into the kitchenette and shone the torch into the sink and against the windows; a moth was fluttering against one of them but there was no other sign of movement. I turned away and the light in my torch suddenly faltered and went out. I crossed to the nearest lamp and examined it; all the connections seemed to be in order, so it must be the bulb or most probably the batteries, and I cursed myself for not having brought any spares. However, I could get some in the morning; I still had the lamps – one lamp at least. When I went up to my bedroom, carefully raising my head above floor level with the lamp held aloft, I found that the second lamp was smoking badly and had nearly gone out. The reason was soon obvious: lack of fuel. I had not realized that they would use so much. I examined the remaining lamp and found that there was barely half an inch of paraffin left in it, not enough to see me through the night. I would have to fill both lamps.

At that moment the bedroom lamp went out and I remembered that I had left the paraffin can on the jetty. I sat on the bed and turned the wick down on my only remaining source of light. Was I going to spend the night in darkness or go and retrieve the can? My fear of the dark competed with my terror of going down those stairs and out onto the jetty. My memory of what had happened that afternoon was still very clear in my mind, too clear. The flame flickered and I knew that I had to come to a decision fast; soon I was going to be in darkness. Was I going to be frightened of merely going downstairs as I had been of testing out the boat? If so, where would it all stop? Soon I would be living in a prison of my own making.

I picked up the lamp and moved towards the open staircase that joined the two floors. The feeble light it cast was only enough to inflame the imagination; every tea chest or article of furniture seemed like the dark shape of an intruder about to spring at me. The fire had burned away to a mere glow in the grate and I crossed to the door that led down to the boat shed. Two hands were needed to open it so I put down the lamp carefully and pulled. The familiar horrible smell invaded my nostrils and a draught fluttered the flame and nearly made it go out. I swung the door open as wide as it would go and peered down the steep flight of stairs; it was like looking down a mine shaft, I could hardly see anything. I paused and then picked up the lamp. I was like a man on the end of a high diving board – the longer I waited, the less likely it was that I would go through with it. I took my first step down and reached out for the slippery wooden rail that ran against the wall. The smell of damp and decay became more pronounced as I descended and I had an irrational notion that I was approaching the entrance to a charnel-house, that on the other side of the door something loathsome was waiting for me. My hand went out and slid back the top bolt. I paused. I almost felt that somebody or something was holding its breath, anticipating the moment when the door would open and I would reveal myself – perhaps not one creature but many: an avenging army awaiting me in the slippery black night.

Almost against my will I sank to my haunches and extended my hand towards the lower bolt. Immediately, a red thong darted beneath the door and reared up to brush against my wrist. I experienced a sharp stinging sensation and, starting back in horror, knocked over the lamp which went out. Gibbering with terror I launched myself at the stairs and scrambled up them in total darkness, imagining that everything I touched was cold and slimy and inhabited by movement. I stumbled through the entrance to the living room and slammed the door shut behind me, feeling relief as the wood bound against the frame. Nothing could get beyond that, I told myself . . . save through the keyhole. I removed the key and twisted the escutcheon into its rightful position. Turning away swiftly I blundered into a carton of books propped on a tea chest and spilled them across the floor. I did not stop but felt my way to the staircase and clambered upstairs as fast as I was able. I did not undress but lay on my bed with a coverlet over me and listened to every sound, every creak, every rattle of a window frame, every cry of a night bird from the marsh outside. What terrified me most was the knowledge that the sound I was listening for in the darkness could never be heard. Has anybody ever heard a worm moving? Extending its body to crawl upstairs, swaying its head to seek out the best route. Worms present the most vivid and terrifying visual images but they make no noise. They even eat silently.

I have no idea how long it was before I fell asleep but it was nine o'clock when I awoke, an unusually late hour for me. The bright East Anglian light streamed through the windows and fears that had seemed insurmountable in the darkness now seemed only ridiculous. I swung my feet to the floor and immediately heard a knock at the front door. I ran my fingers through my hair and tried to smooth out my wrinkled clothing, then went downstairs. As I crossed towards the door I discovered that it was the encyclopedias, the parting gift from my old colleagues, that I had bumped into the night before. One of them had fallen so that it had come open with the pages folded beneath it. I picked it up as I passed and found my eye caught by the section it had fallen open at: WORMS.

I think that my heart must have stopped beating for a couple of seconds – certainly I experienced a feeling of shock that nearly made me drop the book. Only another sharp rat-tat-tat on the door pulled me to my senses.

I put the book down and went to the door. Two men in faded blue overalls looked at me without interest; they were from the council, they said, and they had come to connect the water. I thanked them and stood aside for them to enter the house. Presumably, I said, once they had done their bit, the electrical work could be finished, the immersion heater and that kind of thing. They imagined that it could. I left them working and went out through the side door onto the marsh. I would have liked a cup of tea but that could be my reward when the water was connected. It occurred to me that I could have lit the primus stove as a last resort the night before. All the time that I was trying to think about these inconsequential details I was avoiding thinking about the million-to-one chance of fate that had led to the encyclopedia falling as it did. Not for the first time and not for the last, I felt that I was in the grip of forces far beyond my understanding.

I started to walk across the marsh and followed a path which soon met up with the channel that led to my house. The tide had gone out and I could see that the muddy banks were pitted with worm casts; they looked like an epidemic of smallpox stretching as far as the eye could see along both banks. It was as if the worms were congregating about my house. The cry of a seabird grated menacingly above my head and I turned on my heel and started back towards the house. I suddenly decided that I wanted some human company.

When I arrived on the doorstep the men were leaving. They said that everything was now connected and refused my offer of a cup of tea. I was left alone.

I lit the primus and found that my eye kept straying to the encyclopedia with the crumpled page. What had I got to lose by reading it? It was broad daylight. I was not a necromancer poring over a book of spells by candlelight. The only kettle that I had was an electric one so it was obvious that I would have to boil some water in a saucepan to make the tea. I selected one and held it under the tap; at last something was working. The dream of actually having a bath would soon be a luxurious reality. I turned the tap and there was a shuddering noise followed by an explosion of water into the saucepan; I looked down and saw that it was full of worms. The shock made me drop the saucepan into the sink and the worms reared up just as they had done in the estate agent's office and then weaved towards the plug hole. I struck at them with the saucepan and crushed two before the others had escaped. Again that pungent odour filled the air. I was sure now that it was what I had smelt the night before at the bottom of the stairs to the jetty. I ran the tap again and nothing but water came out. I flushed the writhing remnants of the crushed worms down the sink and pressed home the plug. The worms must have got into the pipes before they were finally connected . . . either that or they had entered from the inside of the house. The last thought made me shiver: could they really have got into the house? Were they like some invisible but all-pervasive roach that could suddenly materialize at will?

I examined a saucepan full of water before putting it on the primus and made myself a cup of tea. Not surprisingly, perhaps, it tasted strange. Of course, it was my imagination but it made me realize how the worms were taking a hold on my life – I had hardly been able to sleep because of them and now the very food I ate seemed threatened. It was difficult for me to stay in this place and not be conscious of them every waking moment. I tipped the unfinished tea into the sink and sat down on a chair in the middle of the room. My eye was still drawn to the encyclopedia. What terrors could the printed word hold that I would be incapable of facing up to after my recent experiences? I got up and brought the book over to the chair.

'WORM,' I read, 'a popular term for animals generally

recalling the familiar earthworm but whose only common feature is an elongated form with bilateral symmetry. The term has therefore no exact scientific meaning.' I reflected upon this statement and then read on to discover the many different kinds of creatures united under the terminology of 'worm': flat worms, parasitic flukes, tapeworms, roundworms, pinworms, pigworms, eelworms, marine bristle-worms, leeches, thorny-headed worms, horse-hair worms, wireworms, bagworms, bollworms, tongueworms, redworms, hookworms, gapeworms, eyeworms, lungworms, threadworms, whipworms and many more. By the time I had come to the end of this grisly list and read of some of their habits and the depredations they caused among animals and human life, I felt physically nauseated. If my stomach had not been empty I would have vomited. I let the book drop to the floor and stood up, experiencing a sudden wave of giddiness. I sat down again and closed my eyes – not a wise thing to have done. A phantasmagoria of ghastly, writhing objects rose from the pages of the discarded encyclopedia and swirled around in my imagination. Worms, grubs, larvae of every shape and size burst through walls of mortifying flesh and distended entrails. I saw hell by Hieronymus Bosch and worse; all the images of the solicitor's office and the tomb in the village church whirled round and round as if in the mouth of a maelstrom, a mouth that slowly took on human shape. Two nostrils, two eyes appeared above it as it tipped into recognizable view: it was my wife opening her mouth wider to choke down this putrescence. The hydra of tentacles thrashed wildly and then started to slide down her throat. I began to scream.

When the front door opened I stopped. I opened my eyes to see a handsome, hard-faced, middle-aged woman staring down at me in surprise and alarm. She looked round the room anxiously. 'Are you all right? What's the matter then?'

'A nightmare,' I blurted. 'I slept very badly last night – I must have dropped off again. I'm sorry if I alarmed you.'

'You're the one who sounded alarmed,' she said. There

was a silence whilst I stood up and tried to stop trembling. 'Mr Hildebrand—?'

'That's right. What can I do for you?' As I spoke it suddenly occurred to me that I had seen the woman before somewhere. I was only just coming to my senses.

'I'm Mrs Mullins. Mrs Valentine said you might need me.' My expression showed that I was still none the wiser. 'I clean up at the house.'

'Of course. It's Betty Mullins, isn't it?' I recalled that Mrs Valentine had only mentioned a Christian name.

'That's right. I did see you passing one time that I were at the house.'

'Yes, well . . .' I started to pull myself together. 'I would be grateful for some assistance. Could you manage two mornings a week? Afternoons if that would be easier.'

'I'd prefer afternoons. I usually go to Mrs Valentine in the morning.'

'Perfect,' I said. 'I'm afraid things are a bit primitive at the moment. They've only just—' I broke off because I had suddenly realized where I had seen the woman before. Going into Wilson's cottage. I could not be positive but I was pretty certain. I saw her looking at me uneasily and pressed on. 'They've only just connected the water. There's still no electricity.'

She was still looking at me strangely and I felt a fresh start of anxiety. Had Wilson passed on his suspicions to her? 'I might be able to help you there,' she said slowly. 'My old man works for the Eastern Electricity Board.'

My face lit up. The news was doubly interesting to me. Most importantly it meant that Mrs Betty Mullins was not a permanent fixture in the Wilson cottage; if she had been there for a few hours of stolen love the evening before, it was unlikely that she would be a visitor tonight. I would have to take advantage of her absence to pay a call. 'You mean, your husband might be able to pull a few strings?' I said innocently. 'I'd be very grateful if he could.'

'I could ask him, anyway,' she said. 'He's on the installation

side and he does a lot of private work, wiring and that.' She
gave me a sharp look and I realized what she was getting at.
Employ her husband on a freelance basis and I could find him
more cooperative in his E.E.B. capacity. It occurred to me that
the Mullinses were probably quite a canny couple. Village life
in north Norfolk was perhaps less rustic and innocent than I
had first imagined it.

'Well, there are a few things I want doing,' I said. 'I'd like a
light down those back stairs for instance. And something out
in the boathouse wouldn't be a bad idea.'

'Bring the birds in,' she said.

Her words struck me like a slap round the face. 'What do
you mean?'

'Light attracts birds that fly at night. You'll bring them in off
the marshes if you leave it on for long. Mr Valentine used to
find it a problem when he was working down there.'

'That's probably why he rigged up a piece of netting,' I said.
'I found the remains of some birds that had been caught in it.'

Mrs Mullins nodded briskly. 'Most likely.' There was no
trace of compassion in her voice. I began to feel that she was a
tough and self-sufficient woman.

'What did Mr Valentine use to do here?'

'Metal work, mostly.' She preferred no further information
but glanced round at the packing cases in the room as if assess-
ing their weight. 'Do you want me to come in this afternoon
then? I expect you'll have unpacked most of this lot.' The last
sentence was uttered with sufficient force as to make it almost
an order. For a second I was reminded of my wife.

'Yes, do come,' I said. 'I should have made some work for
you by then. And I'd like to talk to your husband too.'

'I'll ask him to come round this evening.'

'This evening may be a bit difficult. Could he come round
tomorrow?' Giving the impression of being slightly put out,
she said that she would see, and promptly made a flat statement of her hourly rate. It was a sum I could just afford and, if
I was honest with myself, the idea of having a cleaning woman

rather appealed – having a house in the country and what might
be described, though never to her face, as a servant, I was now
almost the country gentleman. A considerable elevation from
pushing an ancient Hoover round a small London flat.

I now felt less worried that Wilson might have passed on
any suspicions he felt about me to Mrs Mullins. She was not
the kind of woman who inspired confidences nor would she
have inspired much trust in me had she been possessed of any.
I felt that she and Wilson were probably two of a kind, united
perhaps by some bond of lust, but for the rest independent
and self-seeking. Perhaps this was their attraction to each
other. An attachment based on mutual distrust can often be a
strong one.

Mrs Mullins returned shortly after two o'clock, by which
time I had dutifully unpacked the contents of most of the tea
chests. The encyclopedias I placed on a top shelf, vowing that
I would never open one of them again. I had kept a lookout
for Wilson in the garden but there was no sign of him, nor of
Mrs Valentine. I imagined that she was discreetly keeping out
of the way whilst I settled in. Mrs Mullins launched herself
unasked at the windows with a rag and a bottle of cleaning
fluid and I tried to conquer my distaste and force myself to eat
something. The emergence of the worms from the tap had
left me with the feeling that everything was contaminated, a
feeling exacerbated by what I had read in the encyclopedia.
I felt that anything I touched or ate might be a means of
introducing worms into my own system, that every surface
crawled with minute organisms waiting to thrive inside me.
In the back of my throat there was always the queasy taste of
incipient nausea; the thought of eating or drinking anything
repulsed me. Nevertheless I knew that I must eat to live, that I
was being irrational.

I opened the kitchen cupboard and the first thing that met
my eyes was a garishly labelled tin of spaghetti. I looked at
the illustration showing serpentine strands in a thick, orange
sauce and immediately began to gag. I ran to the lavatory and

was painfully sick. Fortunately Mrs Mullins was in another
part of the house, but she entered the room shortly afterwards. She was holding one of the lamps and it only helped
me to remember that another night was approaching and that
the can of paraffin was still down on the jetty. Even in daylight
I felt incapable of retrieving it; I could feel a nervous sweat on
my forehead.

'Have you got a fever?' she asked, staring at me closely. 'You
look very pale.'

'I think I may have,' I said. I glanced at my watch. 'I've got
to go out – I have an appointment. Can you fill both the lamps?
There's a can of paraffin in the boathouse.' I hardly gave her
time to reply but took my raincoat and hurried from the
house. My car stood alone in the drive, so I assumed that Mrs
Valentine had gone out. I had no sooner started the engine
than I realized that I had left the torch behind. It would have
been a simple matter to return for it but I released the hand
brake and drove down the drive; I did not want to go back until
Mrs Mullins had braved the jetty. If there was anything still
lurking down there I preferred that she should be the one to
encounter it.

I drove to a hardware store in Hunstanton and bought a
quantity of disinfectant and scouring crystals, as well as a new
torch; I was not prepared to guess the size of the batteries for
the old one and discover, too late, that I had made a mistake.
I also visited the hotel where I had taken tea with my wife. I
chose this because I remembered that there were wash-basins
in the toilets. I scrubbed my hands and held them under the
hot tap until they were red and I could bear the heat no longer.
Then I ordered tea. It was not an easy meal to eat and several
times I choked as my disturbed imagination fed involuntarily
on some detail of the food that was placed before me: the
seeds in a slice of cucumber became a profusion of unhatched
eggs; a dusting of desiccated coconut on the iced surface of a
cake seemed like a cluster of small, white maggots. The imagination when once set in motion can prove a terrifying scourge.

I returned home after the hour that Mrs Mullins was supposed to leave and found she had left me a note: 'I could not open door at top of stares so was not able to fetch paraffin.'

I cursed out loud and not at the spelling. I must have slammed the door so tightly shut in my panic that it had jammed. I approached it and noticed that the escutcheon had been moved to one side; presumably Mrs Mullins had done this. However, in my present mood I was not prepared to be certain of anything; I fetched a hammer and two tacks and fixed one on either side of the small metal plate so that it could not be moved. I then set to with the products I had bought in Hunstanton. The scouring crystals I held at arm's length and poured into the drains of the downstairs sink and the bathroom basin; choking fumes filled the air and after a few minutes I flushed the crystals away with cold water. Any worm that stood in their path I knew would be burnt to nothing, and the act gave me a vengeful satisfaction. I was carrying the war to the enemy. I would not be menaced in my own home. Not in daylight, anyway.

The basins cleansed, I took the disinfectant and entered the lavatory. The seat cover was down and I lifted it only to let it drop sharply: a mass of worms was clinging to the inside of the bowl, and the water below was solid with them. Repulsed and terrified I feverishly unscrewed the top from the bottle of disinfectant and slammed the seat and its cover back against the cistern; half a dozen worms that were clinging to the underside of the seat cover dropped to the floor. I slopped disinfectant haphazardly and the worms on the inside of the bowl dropped into the water. The whole mass started to writhe like maggots in a tin and I pulled the chain. Most of them were sucked away but a few new ones appeared and I noticed that some of the most tenacious had taken refuge under the lip of the bowl. I killed everything that I saw moving and flushed again. As in the estate agent's office the worms were terrifyingly adept at melting into any shelter that provided itself. Soon I could see nothing save the brown stain of the disinfectant and one or two livid smears. Only the pungent, stomach-turning odour, more powerful even than that of the disinfectant, spoke emphatically of the presence of the worms.

Eager to escape from the place, I flushed again and slopped more disinfectant into the bowl, before lowering the covers and retreating from the room. I was shaking and my breath came in irregular spurts. What I had seen and fought against had been made doubly horrible by the fact that it was a physical representation of something I had previously seen in my imagination. It was terrifying to believe that I had the power to create the demons which tormented me, that the most awful nightmare could take on a physical form.

CHAPTER SIX

I left Marsh Cottage soon after dark feeling that I was escaping from a medieval castle under siege. Fire and brimstone were ready to rain down on all attackers who showed their noses above the battlements. I had not dared venture down to the jetty but there had been neither sound nor movement from the back stairs. It was almost a relief to be setting off in pursuit of a more tangible quarry. The rain had stopped and a whole patch of the sky was clear. I could see stars and the new moon looking like small, bright islands in a wide ocean bordered by mountains of darkening cloud. I crunched down the drive and saw that Mrs Valentine had returned; her car was near mine and there were lights on in Marsh House. It occurred to me that we had never discussed garaging arrangements – I must choose a moment to raise the subject because if I was expected to park my car on the marsh side of the house the depredations of the salt-laden winds would soon put paid to the bodywork. I was having trouble enough starting it in the damp atmosphere as it was.

I emerged from the gate and set off towards the village. I was glad to be out in the open and felt that I could scent finer weather in the wind. Intimations of summer. On the straight road one could see cars coming from a long way away and I had time to duck down by the side of the ditch so as to remain unobserved; I did not want any good-natured soul stopping to offer me a lift and thus being in a position to reveal that I had not spent the evening at home.

I came to the path and the lay-by was empty. Once again I thought of the police car and felt uneasy. The policeman I had seen could only have been going to see Wilson – Wilson who was officially supposed to be a sick man but who was quite

capable of receiving visitors at his front door. What did he
have to talk to the police about?

I entered the tunnel of overlapping saplings that formed the
path and steered my way between the pools of silver left over
from the rains. The cottage loomed up suddenly and I paused
by the front gate. The light showed in the window just as it
had done on the previous evening. I held my watch up to the
moon and saw that it was within five minutes of when Mrs
Mullins had arrived the night before. I waited for ten minutes
in case she chose to appear again and heard two cars going
past at the end of the path. It now seemed past the hour at
which anyone would call. Anyone but me. I decided to give
it another five minutes and was rewarded by a noise from the
cottage followed by a male exclamation of anger. It sounded
as if Wilson had knocked something over – I was glad to know
that he was at home. I had some gloves in my pocket and I
pulled these on and opened the garden gate. At that stage I
had no plan of action in my mind but I was prepared for any
eventuality: when you have killed somebody it is foolish not
to be. I walked up the path and paused by the front door. In
such circumstances it would be normal to hear a television or
at least a wireless but there was not a sound. I waited a few
moments and then tapped. Nothing happened. I banged on
the door more firmly. This time there was the sound of a door
opening and a gruff voice shouted 'Who's there?'

'James Hildebrand,' I called. 'I've moved in to Mrs Valentine's stables. I've come to see how you are.'

How false those last eight words sounded. I was reminded
of what I had called out to my wife at the sluice gate.

There was another pause and then the sound of a bolt sliding back and a key turning in the lock. The door opened on a
chain and I could see Wilson's unshaven face peering at me.
His breath smelt strongly of alcohol. He looked past me as if
to make sure that I was alone and then unhooked the chain.
'Mr Hildebrand. What an honour.' His tone was openly con-
temptuous. He pulled the door open and stood to one side.

'Come in. I thought we'd be having a chat sooner or later.' I
entered a narrow, scruffy corridor that had two doors leading
off it. Wilson bolted the door behind me; he saw me watching
him and smiled evilly. 'You can't be too careful. The police
advise it.' It was on the tip of my tongue to follow up the reference to police but I decided against it. Wilson indicated a room
on the right of the corridor from which light was coming. 'In
there.'

The room was sleazy and dirty, the furniture cheap and
garish. It was all modern and bore no relation to its surroundings which were plastered walls with the laths showing
and a sagging ceiling with a huge damp patch in one corner
– twentieth-century tat in a sixteenth-century labourer's cottage. The most incongruous element was the illuminated fish
tank against one wall. Bubbles splayed upwards and small,
brightly coloured tropical fish alternately meandered and
darted between weeds and replicas of underwater cottages
and gnomes in diving masks. There was an electric fire with an
artificial flame and log effect in the grate and another smaller,
more conventional model propped on a shelf near the fish
tank. Despite the heating the damp so clearly present in the
room was not held at bay, and the atmosphere was clammy.

Wilson wore a dirty white collarless shirt and a pair of
stained blue pin-stripe trousers that must have once belonged
to a suit. Somebody else's at a guess. His face was sallow and
shiny and he did not look well.

'I expected to find you in bed,' I said.

'Did you?' he said disbelievingly. 'I notice you didn't bring
me anything.' On the shelf below the fish tank were half a
dozen empty beer bottles and some miniatures of spirits. He
clumsily picked up a quarter bottle of Martell brandy and
emptied the remnants into a dirty tumbler. 'I expect you drink
out of full bottles,' he said scornfully.

'I don't drink very much at all,' I said calmly.

'I expect you have to keep your wits about you,' jibed
Wilson. If not drunk he was approaching it and his move-

ments were exaggerated and clumsy. He wagged a finger at me. 'I think I could make life very difficult for you.'

My pulse quickened. 'What do you mean?'

'What do I mean? What do I mean?' He repeated the words like a parrot. 'You know what I mean. That's why you're here.' I said nothing, knowing that he would continue. 'That poor wife of yours. You didn't get on very well, did you?'

'I don't know what you're talking about,' I said.

'Oh yes you do. I heard you, you see. When I was working in the garden and you drove round the back.' My heart sank. 'I can remember your words: "If you don't help me buy this place you'll regret it." Shouting you were.' I kept my silence. 'I wonder what the police would make of that in the circumstances.'

'If you were eavesdropping you must have misheard,' I said, trying to sound as casual as possible. 'My wife wasn't feeling very well as I recall it. She didn't want to get out of the car.'

Wilson emptied his glass emphatically. 'What about later on?' I felt a sharp stab of fear; the expression in my eyes must have been obvious. Wilson's tone was gloating as he continued. 'I was out on the marsh, wasn't I. Setting a few traps. I heard you having a right old up and downer – calling you all the names under the sun she was. And that bit about you not getting your hands on her money. Now that was very interesting. Just think, half an hour later she was dead. I should have followed you, shouldn't I? I bet I'd have seen something interesting.'

I said nothing but looked round the room. I honestly believe that if my eye had hit on something that could have been used as a weapon I would have snatched it up and tried to dash the scoundrel's brains out – a stupid, pathetic gesture because even though in his cups he was probably stronger than I. My spontaneous reaction was not so much against the creature before me but against fate. How unfair it was! Spied on not once but twice.

'I did you a favour, didn't I?' I could think of nothing to say and he nudged my arm. 'Still, I'm a friendly cove. I've suffered a bit at women's hands myself.' He broke off and was shaken by a violent fit of coughing; he clutched his stomach and gasped for breath, and from the expression on his face it was clear that he was in severe pain. The spasm passed and his breathing slowly became normal. Perhaps the man was ill after all. He took the brandy bottle and shook it irritably so that a few drops sprinkled into the bottom of his glass. 'I'll do anybody a favour who does me one.' His tone suggested the opposite of his words. It was grim and menacing.

'I've still no idea what you're getting at,' I said.

This time my arm was gripped hard just above the elbow. 'Oh yes you have. If I'd have told the police what I heard they'd have had you in a little room and they wouldn't have let you out until you signed a confession. I could still shop you if I wanted to.' My arm was tossed aside.

'I suppose it could look bad,' I said meekly.

'Very bad,' said Wilson emphatically. He gripped his stomach as if anticipating another coughing fit but nothing happened. 'Like I said, I reckon you owe me a favour.' He moved his hand to his chest and rubbed it thoughtfully whilst he looked me in the eyes with his head tilted to one side – like a bird listening for a worm, I thought to myself.

'What do you want?' As I spoke I knew that I was biding my time. Wilson had signed his own death warrant before he tried to blackmail me; he had heard too much and if his present bibulous condition was an example of how he passed his evenings then there was no telling when he might blurt it out.

'I think a bit of money mightn't go down amiss. Your wife had some, didn't she? That's why you're living in that place. I think I deserve a little inheritance.'

'My wife left a very small sum,' I said. 'It was swallowed up in the house.'

'I don't think you're too badly off,' said Wilson knowingly. 'A tenner a week wouldn't break you.'

'Ten pounds?' I exclaimed.

'You don't have to act with me,' said my tormentor. 'I know you're a gifted performer. I was watching you down the sluice gate, remember.' He stepped back towards the wall. 'Tell you what, boy. I'll give you something for your money.' He bent down and flipped back a dirty orange rug and a section of threadbare carpet. He inserted his forefinger in a knothole and hoicked up a section of floorboard. Gleaming in the darkness I could see the brilliant multicoloured plumage of a pheasant lying beside a brace of partridges. 'I'll keep you supplied with game. That'll regularize our little arrangement. You won't be my only customer but you'll be paying a little above the market price.'

'So you poach as well,' I said.

Wilson dropped the floorboard back into place and pulled the carpet over it. 'I've done time for it. You know, I had a copper round here last night. Just checking that my gun was licensed, that's what he said. I think he expected to find me standing up to my knees in feathers.' He laughed derisively and the laugh turned into another coughing fit. The sweat was showing through his shirt and he went to stand before the heater near the fish tank. His flesh glistened.

'Ten pounds a week,' I repeated.

'Cheap at the price.' He reached out and took an old mustard tin from beside the fish tank. As I watched with mounting distaste he removed the perforated lid and delved inside with two fingers. They emerged holding a wriggling red worm.

Wilson turned his head and saw my expression. 'What's the matter, don't you like worms?' He nodded towards the fish tank. 'These fellows do.' He held the worm just above the surface so that its tail dangled against the water. Immediately, half a dozen small fish sped to the surface and the worm was torn in half. He fed the remains of the worm through his fingers and the performance was repeated as the fish ate it, section by section until there was nothing left. I watched, repulsed at first, but then with a sudden start of interest. The electric fire was on a shelf above and to the left of the tank. There was one point in the wall with an adapter that held the plugs for the tank and the fire. I remembered my wife pointing out to me an article in the paper about a man who had been electrocuted when his electric fire toppled into the bath with him.

Wilson took anther worm and dangled it over the water. It wriggled desperately and tried to wind itself round his finger. Angrily he began to squeeze it so that bits dropped into the water. The fish darted up and fought over the pieces. If only Wilson would put his hand into the tank ... It was tantalizing to have this opportunity so close but not to be able to profit by it.

'What do you say then?' said Wilson. 'I don't think you have much choice.'

'No, I suppose I don't,' I said, humouring him. I had my hands grasped together in front of me as I often do at moments of stress, and I suddenly felt my wedding ring. I had kept it on for no other reason than that over the years it had become painfully difficult to remove. Now, as another worm was dismembered, I struggled to remove it without attracting his attention.

'You never want to overfeed them,' said Wilson. 'If the food starts decomposing that can start off a disease.'

I gritted my teeth and forced the ring over the swollen knuckle, painfully bending back my thumb nail. 'I'm a bit short of cash at the moment,' I said. 'How about this taking care of a few instalments.' I tossed the ring into the tank and it zig-zagged to the bottom with two striped fish quickly in attendance. Their noses quivered against it for a second and then they turned away disappointed.

'You daft booger,' said Wilson. 'What did you do that for?' He peered through the side of the tank.

'It's solid gold,' I lied. 'Twenty-four carat. Cost over fifty pounds when I bought it. Must be worth a lot more now – at least a hundred probably.'

The ring was half-buried in the sand at the bottom of the tank, just beside a cracked china mermaid. Wilson licked his lips.

'Who are you trying to kid?' he said. He started to roll up his sleeve and I turned my head away; I could not look him in the eye. My hands were starting to shake and I thought he must see them and suspect something. Instead, he was only thinking about the ring. 'I guarantee that's not worth what you say you paid for it.' He carefully inserted his arm into the tank up to the elbow.

I had realized when killing my wife that hesitation could be dangerous and this time I did not hold back. My hand shot up and I knocked the fire off the shelf and towards the tank. At the same instant I threw myself sideways. There was a blinding flash that seemed to fill the whole room and a piercing shriek of pain that dominated every other sound. The lights went off and for a terrifying second I thought that I myself was dead. Wilson's scream seemed to be going on and on through my head without stopping and I could still see the jagged white flame even with my eyes tightly closed.

Eventually the sound died away as if down a long tunnel and I became aware of the smell of burning. It was not a smell I had experienced before and I was forced to accept that this strange, singed odour must be given off by Wilson's body. I sat on the floor with my back against the damp wall and hoped that he was dead. A sudden sound of movement made my heart leap towards my mouth. Then I realized that it was the fish slithering around on the floor; another noise turned out to be the bars of the electric fire in the grate contracting as they cooled. I felt in my pocket and brought out my torch: I was frightened in the dark yet I had no great desire to see what the light revealed.

Wilson lay with his hand still inside the fallen tank and the fire resting against his face. His eyes were open and staring with a terrible intensity and his chest and head were spattered with wet sand. The fish lay gulping, their eyes already dead; occasionally one would skip in the air before lying still again. I felt sorry for them but there was nothing I could do.

The object I noticed with most repugnance was the tin that

had held the worms. It was now lying on its side amongst the
debris. I crawled forward on my hands and knees and gingerly
extended a hand to feel Wilson's chest; if there was a heartbeat
I could not find it. I tried one of the wrists with the same result.
Now what I needed was to recover my ring. I shone the torch
amongst the welter of cheap ornaments still piled up in the
corner of the tank but it did not seem to be there. I began to
panic and found a cheap biro with which I began to poke around
in the mess of weed and bric-a-brac. There was no sign of the
ring. I looked among the dying fish and searched diligently all
over the floor where I found the now broken mermaid. Wilson
had fallen on a strip of carpet and there was no possibility that
the ring had slipped beneath the floorboards. With mounting
exasperation I began to believe that it must be beneath his
body; whatever happened I would have to move it to make sure
and that would risk rousing suspicions when the police came
to investigate. I nearly cursed out loud. The position of the
corpse was perfect at the moment, giving a clear indication of
what must have happened: a precariously positioned fire had
been dislodged into the aquarium by a man probably made
clumsy by drink. A tragic accident but not unique.

I lowered myself nearer to the floor and shone my torch
into every nook and cranny. As I did so, something glinted at
me from the worm tin. I quickly emptied it in my hand and
received half a dozen worms and my ring. Dropping the can I
snatched the ring and tried to shake the worms from my hand;
two of them clung as if bound by an adhesive and I was forced
to pull them away from my skin and scrape them off against
one of the shelves. I was now thoroughly unnerved and shaking and sobbing – to have killed a man was ghastly enough
without this. I was half way to the door before I remembered
the tin that I had dropped on the floor; it would have my
fingerprints on it. I returned and wiped it scrupulously with a
handkerchief. I thought that I had struck the electric fire with
the side of my hand but I took no chances and wiped that also.
All the time I was trying to keep calm and think of everything

that needed to be done, every trace that had to be covered. I had only taken my gloves off to remove my ring so there was nothing that I had touched bare-handed save the tin and, possibly, the fire. I pulled on my gloves and stepped over the corpse. Only one fish was still moving, its mouth opening and shutting rhythmically.

I approached the front door and paused. It was clearly Wilson's habit to lock himself in securely at night. Despite my anxiety to get away from the place, I went back down the corridor and into the room on the left. This led to a low scullery with a back door and beside it a chipped, old-fashioned sink with an iron-framed casement window behind. There were dirty dishes in the sink and a row of grime-smeared washing products along the sill, some of them so old that I hardly recognized the design of the packets. The window opened outwards with a catch that swung sideways into a slit in the jamb. The back door was locked with the key on the inside.

I returned to the front door and slid home the bolt and connected the chain. Now it was completely locked as it had been when I arrived at the cottage. I went back to the scullery and moved some of the plates in the sink so that I could use it as a stepping stone to the window. I also carefully set aside the containers on the sill, noticing where each had been. Now I opened the window and shone my torch down till I found a brick-edged drain opening that would save me from leaving a tell-tale footprint on the still wet ground. I climbed into the sink and then, carefully, over the sill and down onto the drain surround. It was a feat I would have found a good deal easier a few years back when my body was more supple, but expediency is a great motivator and I was soon outside with my breathing hardly disturbed. I turned on a tap to rinse my footprints away and replaced the greasy plates in the sink. The washing products I rearranged one by one so they were standing in the same circles of dust-free sill as before. A drop of water had materialized on one cap and I carefully dabbed it away with my handkerchief.

Now came the difficult part. I folded back the securing rod against the frame and held it above the level of the holding spike as I gently closed the window. When my fingers were becoming pinched I manoeuvred the rod onto the spike and turned my attention to the swinging catch half way up the frame. This I pushed back until it pressed against the jamb when the window was almost closed. I tapped gently and the catch scraped back against the wood until it swung into its slot. The securing rod had not slotted onto the spike but this would have been almost too much to hope for. I tried to pull at the window but it would not budge; to all intents and purposes the house was locked from the inside. The thought gave me a fresh start of alarm as I imagined the consequences should I have left something incriminating behind. The fears receded when I thought calmly for a few moments and assured myself that this was not the case. I stepped carefully onto the damp earth and away into the night.

CHAPTER SEVEN

It was several days before the body was discovered. I remained in a considerable state of suspense but comforted myself with the thought 'the longer the better'. If there were any queries about the cause of death then the more advanced the state of decomposition the more difficult it would be for the true facts to be ascertained.

Eventually the news was brought to me by Mrs Valentine who had heard it from Betty Mullins and rung the police to confirm that it was true. Apparently the police had gone to Wilson's cottage after he had not been seen at any of his usual haunts and had failed to keep an appointment with a wild-fowling acquaintance. They had received no answer to repeated banging on doors and windows and had eventually forced their way in via the kitchen window – this detail afforded me considerable comfort, as their entry would almost certainly have obliterated any clues that I had left when leaving. Wilson's body had been found sprawled out in the sitting room, where it appeared that he had electrocuted himself when doing something to his fish tank. An added touch of unpleasantness was contributed by the fact that a cache of maggot-infested game was found underneath the floorboards. There were also some details of the state of his body that Mrs Valentine shuddered to reveal and which I did not press for.

I expressed what I hoped was the right amount of horror and sympathy and said that if there was any help I could give I would gladly give it. This offer, of course, I made in the full knowledge that it would not be accepted. Mrs Valentine said that I was most kind and asked if I could dispense with Mrs Mullins's services for the day as she was most distressed by the news and wanted to go home. I said that I quite understood.

Subsequently there was an inquest and a verdict of 'accidental death' was recorded. I went to the funeral – I thought it was the least I could do. I remember standing at the back of the almost empty church and watching the sunlight shine through the stained glass windows behind the altar. Summer was coming in and I had already enjoyed many fine walks across the marshes and along the seashore. It was certainly true that the weather had a great influence on one's moods, here particularly.

I still kept up my precautions against the worms – the scouring crystals and the disinfectant – but it was a long time since I had seen one in the house. I was beginning to think that they were a seasonal thing or perhaps a one-off manifestation that would never happen again. I even went down to the boathouse by myself without qualm, although I chose not to do so after dark. There were certain memories that I knew would never go away. My eyes drifted sideways as the vicar's voice droned on and lighted on the carved relief of the worms of hell on the side of the tomb. How cleverly they were done – one could almost swear that there was a tremor of movement in the stone. Strange that this particular form of imagery should be employed here. I had never seen it used anywhere else.

My eyes moved on down the aisle to the cheap coffin that contained the remains of Wilson – William Thomas Wilson as I now knew him to have been christened. With his death and the disappearance of the worms I felt that a great weight was lifted from my shoulders. Now I was free from fear and I could begin to enjoy my life at Blanely.

How wrong I was.

PART II

CHAPTER EIGHT

'I think it's disgraceful,' said Mrs Hovell. 'Quite disgraceful. We ought to get up a petition.'

'It's going to take more than a petition to stop it,' said Mrs Hughes grimly. 'We need one of those fighting committees that they have when they're going to build airports.'

The conversation was taking place as I entered the village shop, a dark, timbered room that looked as if the black beams were resting on the piles of biscuits, breakfast cereals and tinned beans that filled every corner, hardly leaving space for people to pay newspaper bills and draw their old age pensions.

The two women turned on me and nodded a brisk greeting. 'What do you think, Mr Hildebrand?' To be greeted by my name was a mark of acceptance that it had taken me the best part of a year to earn. Summer and autumn had passed, and we were now in the bleak, post-Christmas trough when nature seemed to have ground to a halt and one despaired of ever feeling warm sunshine against the cheek or seeing a bud come to flower.

'What is it?' I said. 'The marina?'

'The marina!' Mrs Hovell made a sharp clicking noise with her tongue and tossed her head scornfully. 'That's not a marina they're going to build.'

Mrs Hughes leant across the counter and projected her voice like a bullet. 'It's a nuclear reactor.'

I was rendered speechless; the idea seemed so implausible as to be almost ridiculous. A nuclear reactor? Here? They were always in Scotland or somewhere miles away from anywhere . . . A moment's rational thought followed: Blanely *was* miles away from anywhere. I remembered the time I had been on a walk and first seen men with theodolytes on the marsh; I

had immediately asked them what they were doing and the
replies had been evasive: checking the sea defences. I had
accepted that and been no more than mildly annoyed when
a kind of builder's yard was established a mile down the road;
I had noticed the stockpiling of materials and the erection of
workingmen's huts surrounded by a wire fence but paid no
particular attention until workmen started to build a road
across the marshes and lorry-loads of foundation were carried
out to the sea's edge and dumped in untidy piles like refuse.
There was a local outcry and we were told that a private firm
had leased part of the marsh to build a marina. Permission had
been given because it would bring more holidaymakers to the
area and provide work for local people. The harbours in the
local tourist villages were small and overcrowded and it was
difficult to find a mooring, so there seemed a certain logic in
the case for a marina, but it occurred to me now, as I stood
in the village store, that I had never seen anything in writing
about the marina. Nor had the foundation that was being laid
at the water's edge fitted in with my conception of what a
mooring place for yachts would look like. It was not easy to
see too clearly what was happening because a fence had been
built round the site and there were notices saying that the area
was patrolled by guard dogs. I had assumed that this was to
prevent pilfering; now I was not so sure.

Mrs Hovell and Mrs Hughes were still staring at me, waiting for a reaction.

'I can't believe it,' I said.

'It's true. Mrs Bates's boy works at Lynn in the council
offices and he saw the plans. "Nuclear Reactor, Blanely" –
that's what they were marked.'

I was silent. Somebody else came into the shop and I turned
away as the women launched in to her. A nuclear reactor: I
did not really know what it was apart from a means of pro-
ducing power from atomic energy, but the words frightened
me. When I thought of nuclear energy I thought of death
and danger; I saw mushroom clouds and hairless mis-shapen

bodies of radiation victims. I had read of the dangers implicit in harnessing nuclear energy to peaceful needs but I had never believed that it would touch my life. Above all I loathed the thought of some huge, ugly, man-made structure permanently scarring the lonely beauty of the marshes. Would there be columns of smoke soaring into the sky as from a power station? Nauseating odours polluting the wind? Toxic waste matter poisoning the environment?

'The worms aren't going to like this,' I said. I spoke the words out loud without knowing what had brought the thought or its expression into my mind. The three women broke off their conversation and stared at me.

'Beg pardon, Mr Hildebrand?'

'Nothing,' I said hurriedly. 'I was just thinking out loud. It's terrible about the reactor.'

They nodded and went back to their conversation as I began to fill my basket. Occasionally one of them would glance towards me, followed by the other two, and I knew that they were now talking about me. I think I had a reputation for being slightly strange. Country people are great gossips and there was I, living alone yet not so far from the widowed Mrs Valentine; it was not surprising that tongues should wag. I think Betty Mullins carried a lot of gossip back to the village. She could never understand my fetish for scouring the drains; she was always picking up the caustic soda and shaking her head. If she had been a more companionable woman I might have told her about the strange infestation of worms but she always guarded her distance and I did likewise. There was also something sly about her, which made me slightly uneasy in her presence. I knew that she had visited Wilson's cottage after his death but she never came to the funeral. She was a funny woman.

When I left the village shop I took my purchases home and looked out of the living room window across the marshes. Thankfully I could not see the site of the nuclear reactor but knowing it was there, just beyond the sweep of my vision, made my heart ache. The wind rattled the window panes and I wondered what subconscious impulse had made me speak out as I had done in the village store. 'The worms are not going to like this.' I repeated the words and the wind blew harder and bent down the grasses below the window as if forcing them to bow in vigorous assent. I turned round quickly because I had the sudden impression that there was somebody standing behind me but the room was empty. It was a long time since I had had any trouble with my nerves and I put it down to anxiety about the nuclear reactor. The women in the shop might be right; it should not be too late to do something, to form some kind of action group. If people could stop airports being built or force councils to build by-passes, then surely we could at least make them think twice about siting a nuclear reactor on our marshes. What was alarming was the sinister way in which work had been started without any of the locals knowing about it. An outcry must have been anticipated and the authorities had acted with a furtive sense of purpose to get the project under way. This implied a degree of forethought and determination that it would be difficult to combat. The country was desperate for more energy supplies; would the government allow a few isolated nature-lovers in the lonely East Anglian marshes to stand in the way of the needs of millions?

It was in a mood of deepening gloom that I pulled on my wellingtons and set off for a walk across the marshes. I felt that I needed to see what was happening for myself. The cranes loomed up like the spires of a distant cathedral and soon I could see the slab outline of the foundation they were standing on. Construction was racing ahead and I was amazed to see how much had been done since I had last passed by the site. Skeletal fingers of steel poked out of blocks of reinforced concrete and what looked like a huge, squat brick kiln was taking shape.

Any last doubts concerning what I had heard in the village shop vanished: this was no marina. I watched a line of lorries waiting to dump more gravel for the foundation and began to follow the fence round to where a couple of bulldozers were pushing earth over sunken drainage pipes. I had taken only a few steps when a uniformed man holding an alsatian on a short lead materialized from behind a clump of rushes. He asked me where I was going and, when I said I was out for a walk, demanded identification. I told him that I did not have any and he asked where I lived. On hearing the words Marsh Cottage he immediately said my name. I was startled and a little frightened. If they were employing security men who had checked up on everybody in the area, then the authorities certainly meant business. I deemed it unwise to mention anything about nuclear reactors but asked what was being built. The man told me that it was going to be a small power station that would give a substantial boost to existing resources in the area and take the weight off the national grid. It sounded like a prepared response but I did not press for further information; I commented that it looked like rain and turned on my heel. The alsatian sniffed my coat as if making a note of my smell and the guard wrote something in a little book as I walked away. It was an experience that left me with an even greater sense of foreboding.

I decided not to walk back the way I had come but go along the beach. The sky was lowering and there was a storm in the air. After nearly a year in the area I was beginning to be able to read the weather. I trudged along by the dunes with my coat collar turned up and saw that there was a figure ahead. It was a man digging for worms and with a strange sense of *déjà vu* I was reminded of when I had first seen Wilson; perhaps it was this recollection that made me go over to the man so that I could confirm to myself that there was no real similarity. Perhaps, as an adopted local, I wanted to address one of my countrymen after a brush with the common foe.

In fact I did have a vague acquaintance with the man; I had seen him at Wilson's funeral. He was the companion with whom Wilson was supposed to have gone wildfowling and

who had begun to suspect that something might be wrong
when his friend never turned up. I wished him good day and
he grunted and straightened up to scratch his head. 'I don't
understand it.'

I asked him what he did not understand and he indicated
the area of sand dug up about him. 'Look what I turned over.
A good cricket pitch and I haven't lit upon one worm.'

I felt a stirring of unease. 'Is that unusual?'

'Never known anything like it before in my life. And I've been
digging this beach fifty years. I don't know where they've gone.'

'Perhaps there's some disease killing them,' I said. 'Like
myxomatosis with the rabbits.'

'It's possible, I suppose, though they've survived everything
so far. We had a shipload of chemicals go down off here once.
And oil, of course – Lord knows there's been enough of that.
But then you see them, dead mostly, but you still see them.
Now I'm not finding *one*.' He drove his spade almost viciously
into the tightly packed grey sand and I watched apprehen-
sively as he turned it over. A tiny shell glistened like fool's gold
and was scuffed aside. I made some noises that were meant to
express regret and sympathy and went on my way. I did not
find it easy to talk to the local people or, more exactly, to finish
talking to them. To extend a few words of greeting into a conversation required an art I did not possess.

I returned to the dunes and, almost unconsciously, found
myself taking the route that led past the sluice where my wife
had perished. I hesitated and then pressed forward; for some
unknown reason, fears and pressures were starting to build up
inside me and I did not wish to give them too much rein. It was
not only the news of the nuclear reactor; that alone could not
account for my feelings of impending doom.

I passed the block house and saw the scarce-changed outline
of the sluice gates ahead. Half a dozen steps through the tall
marsh grass and I stopped dead. A woman was leaning on the
rail and looking down into the water; silhouetted as she was
against the horizon and with her head tilted away from me,

she looked like only one person who had once been on this earth. I felt as icy cold as if I had been plunged into the water beneath her; after the man on the beach who had reminded me of Wilson this sight was almost unbearable. Something attached itself to my feet and I let out a cry of terror, then looked down and saw that it was Mrs Valentine's remaining King Charles spaniel, the other having died of old age before Christmas. The dog sniffed my boots and then started to wag its tail in recognition. Mrs Valentine stepped down from the parapet and came towards me.

'Mr Hildebrand. What a surprise.' She snapped her fingers at the dog. 'Heel, Ripper! I'm sorry if he alarmed you.'

I was still shaken but I felt foolish at having let the dog disturb me. 'He gave me a shock, that's all,' I said. 'I was thinking about something else. No doubt you've heard all about the nuclear reactor.'

'I have indeed – or as much as anybody has been allowed to hear.' Mrs Valentine started to walk towards the block house, almost driving me before her down the narrow path. I think that she was being diplomatic and taking the initiative in removing us from this particular spot. 'Have you been to see what they're up to?' I described my experiences with the security guard and she shook her head and addressed the dog. 'It doesn't sound like a good walk for us, Ripper. I think that alsatian might fancy you for his supper.' Ripper wagged his tail, delighted to be spoken to. He was nearly blind and it was obvious that he was soon going to go the same way as his erstwhile companion. Mrs Valentine smiled charmingly at me. 'Shall we walk up the beach a little bit and go back via the village? I'm glad to have bumped into you because I wanted to enlist your aid. I imagine you're as horrified by this reactor thing as the rest of the village?'

'Of course,' I said.

'Good. Because I think we've got to set up some kind of a committee. I've already talked to Doctor Parr and Colonel Fraser – you have met Colonel Fraser, haven't you?'

'Fleetingly,' I said. Once in a while, Mrs Valentine would invite local dignitaries to her house for sherry after Sunday matins, and on one of these occasions I had been included in the party and introduced to a florid-faced man who numbered among his other functions that of commander of the local territorial army unit. He had quickly found someone else to talk to after we had exchanged a few words.

'The vicar's sitting on the fence,' continued Mrs Valentine. 'I think he's worried about involving the Church in what he thinks will become a political situation.' She reeled off some other names and I listened dutifully. Mrs Valentine called to the dog which had gone snuffling on down the beach and led the way across the marsh. A snipe rose into the air as if fired from a gun. 'Of course, most of these people have full-time jobs so they won't be able to devote themselves totally to the cause.' She smiled at me again with her pleasant blue eyes. 'You and I are more fortunate in that respect.' She cleared her throat in the way that people do when they are about to ask a favour. 'I was wondering whether you would be prepared to be a sort of secretary to the committee. There's certain to be a lot of paper work – sending out notices and letters and all that kind of thing – and I know you've had a lot of business experience.'

'I'd be delighted,' I said, wishing that I could inject more enthusiasm into my voice. It was difficult to imagine Mrs Valentine leading Doctor Parr, Colonel Fraser and even a fully committed vicar to victory over the concrete monolith I had just visited. Still, perhaps I was giving in too easily. One had to put up a fight.

'We have a lot of powerful interests on our side,' said Mrs Valentine bravely. 'The National Trust will be up in arms and there are a good many influential people who own property round here. I think we can count on a few voices being raised in parliament.'

'The trouble is that it seems to be a *fait accompli*,' I said. 'It's not at the planning stage. They're actually building it.'

A flight of mallard rose from a nearby pool with a small thunderclap of wings and Mrs Valentine called for her dog. 'Ripper! Heel, boy.' The dog did not appear and it occurred to me that I had not seen him since we left the beach. 'Ripper! Ripper! Ripper!' The words echoed away across the marsh almost like the call of a bird. We looked back along the path expectantly. Nothing moved, save the grasses bowing before the wind. 'He's getting old,' said Mrs Valentine. We retraced our steps to the dunes without seeing anything and she began to get anxious, so we went back to the beach and shouted against the noise of the sea. The shore stretched away empty on either side. The man digging for worms had gone and there was only a bulldozer on the horizon moving slowly like a ponderous beetle across the mud.

'He must have followed us and gone into the reeds,' I said.

'Stupid dog.' Mrs Valentine sounded more worried than angry. We went back to the pool where the mallard had risen and began calling again. I pushed into the reeds but the ground soon became soft beneath my feet and the water rose nearly to the top of my boots. Standing on tiptoe, I was able to see a dense thicket of reeds rearing up like an island in the middle of a lagoon of brackish water. It was a dismal place, heavy with a familiar smell of putrefaction. The reeds pressed against me and I began to feel trapped and frightened; I tried to turn back but my feet were wedged deep in the mud. Something moved in the reeds a few yards away and I called the dog's name. The noise stopped at the sound of my voice. In the grip of panic I tore one foot free and felt cold water slopping into the other boot. When I hobbled back to Mrs Valentine I was spattered with mud up to the thighs.

'Your hand,' she said. It was dripping blood and had a ruler-straight cut across the palm where I must have grabbed a reed. I wrapped a handkerchief around it and we continued calling and looking. Mrs Valentine thought that the dog might have been caught in a trap but that did not explain why it was making no noise.

'It's possible that it could have gone into the reeds and had a heart attack,' I said. 'It was old.'

She looked at my boots. 'Perhaps it's trapped in the mud.'

We looked for another half hour without seeing or hearing anything, Mrs Valentine becoming more and more distressed. In the end I suggested that the dog might have gone home and be waiting for us there. I did not think that she believed this any more than I did but it was beginning to get dark and she must have realized that searching this wilderness of reeds was a physical impossibility even in daylight.

We went back to Marsh House and there was no sign of Ripper. I had never seen Mrs Valentine so agitated – the nuclear reactor was forgotten. She said that she would take some food back to the place where we had last seen the dog in case he was wandering around the marshes looking for us. I was sceptical but I decided that it was best to humour her; doing something was much better than waiting helplessly. I accompanied her to the spot where the mallard had risen and we left a plate of cold chicken near the path.

In the morning, the chicken was all gone but there was no sign of the dog. Mrs Valentine was heartened by the disappearance of the food but after a few days had passed she began to give up hope. The dog was never seen again.

CHAPTER NINE

The first meeting of the protest committee was held at Marsh House in the week following the disappearance of Mrs Valentine's dog. I had the opportunity of re-meeting Colonel Fraser and found him scarcely more friendly than on the first occasion. He did most of the talking, with Mrs Valentine filling in the gaps and Doctor Parr listening solemnly and looking as if he was having difficulty keeping his eyes open. The vicar was present but in what he took care to describe as 'a strictly non-executive capacity'. It was decided that the group would be called the 'Save Blanely! Association', with an exclamation mark, and that Mrs Valentine would be chairman – the appellations chairwoman, chairlady and chairperson were rejected after long discussion for reasons that I cannot recall – and that Colonel Fraser would be president. A distinguished patron would be sought from amongst the ranks of the local gentry, and a fighting fund would be set up and a meeting held in the village hall as soon as possible with an invitation extended to the *Eastern Daily Press* and the local member of parliament. Anti-nuclear reactor posters would be printed with a wording to be agreed and a special letter heading designed for all correspondence emanating from the committee. Colonel Fraser stressed the importance of 'looking as though you mean business'.

There was a long discussion about the subscription to be levied and it was eventually decided that it should not be less than 50p for adults and 25p for those below school-leaving age. Collecting boxes would be placed in all the shops in the surrounding villages and Colonel Fraser suggested that the proceeds of a special church collection should be given to the fund. The vicar pursed his lips sceptically and said he would have to consult his bishop on this point; he rather felt that the latter might take the view that the appropriation of the offertory monies would represent a secular intervention into matters ecclesiastical. Colonel Fraser said nothing but pointedly avoided addressing another word to the vicar during the rest of the meeting.

I took notes diligently but all the time, in my mind's eye, I could see fresh slabs of concrete moving into place and hear the growl of the bulldozers as they bit into the earth. Whilst we talked, the reactor was springing up like a mushroom, and it was difficult to believe that anything that was done or said in Mrs Valentine's elegant drawing room was ever going to get it dismantled and the marsh returned to its old state.

When the meeting was over and the Colonel had departed in his Range Rover and the vicar on his bicycle, I took my notes and returned to the cottage. It was one of Mrs Mullins's afternoons and I could hear her coughing as I approached the front door. She had recently begun to look much older and not at all well; she complained of stomach pains and said that nothing the doctor gave her did any good. I sympathized as much as I could but thought that she probably had some indigestion problem made worse by a bad diet. I knew from my own experience that as the years went by the body became more of a liability than a servant.

When I entered the sitting room Mrs Mullins was cleaning upstairs. I called out to her that it was me and walked past her handbag which was lying open on a low table. Something shiny caught my eye and I glanced inside it. Clumsily wrapped in a headscarf were half a dozen antique silver teaspoons. I quickly withdrew one to look at the hall mark – yes, it was genuine.

The discovery made me uneasy and embarrassed. My first thought was that Mrs Mullins must have helped herself to the teaspoons whilst working at Marsh House. I nearly raised the matter with her there and then before realizing that this would be stupid; they might possibly belong to her and she was taking them to be sold or valued, or perhaps Mrs Valentine had given them to her. It was probably best to be discreet and approach Mrs Valentine. I could not let the matter rest.

When Mrs Mullins had gone I returned to Marsh House and rang the front door bell. Mrs Valentine opened it almost immediately as if she had been passing nearby. There was a faint blush on her cheek and she looked slightly discomforted to see me. I noticed that she held the ivory envelope opener in her hand.

'I'm sorry to disturb you,' I said. 'I've just been alerted to something that I think you ought to know about.'

She stepped aside and ushered me into the house. 'About the nuclear reactor?'

'No, something else.'

She saw that my expression was serious and leant forward to touch my arm. 'Not about Ripper?'

'No, no. It concerns Mrs Mullins.'

Mrs Valentine had led the way into the drawing room so that I could not see how her face reacted to this news. She replaced the envelope opener on its tray and turned towards me looking calm and collected. 'What about her?'

'It's rather embarrassing,' I said. 'When she was cleaning the house, I happened to glance inside her handbag – by accident, of course. It contained what I'm fairly certain were half a dozen silver teaspoons.' I paused, waiting for Mrs Valentine to draw the obvious conclusion, but she said nothing. 'I couldn't help wondering if perhaps she'd picked them up here.'

'How odd.' Mrs Valentine looked disapproving and I rather felt that it was me she disapproved of. I began to wish that I had never mentioned the matter – it was no affair of mine anyway. I was being made to feel like someone who told tales out of school. 'Betty Mullins has been with me fifteen years. We've never had any trouble.'

'There's probably a very simple explanation,' I said, eager to find some way of climbing down. 'I just thought I ought to mention it, that's all.'

Mrs Valentine said nothing but crossed to a heavy, carved oak sideboard which dominated one wall of the room. She slid a drawer open and looked inside. 'No, there's nothing missing. Nothing at all.' She slid the drawer closed and turned to face me, a haughty expression on her face.

'I am relieved. I hope I haven't caused you any distress by raising the matter.'

Before Mrs Valentine could answer, the telephone in the hall started to ring. She excused herself and went out. I heard her say 'Oh yes, vicar,' in a voice that sounded as if she was resigning herself to a long conversation. The door was half-closed and she could not see me from where she was standing. On an impulse I crossed to the sideboard and pulled open the drawer; the interior was divided into a number of dark blue plush-lined sections, each of them equipped to receive a set of cutlery. Nearly half the sections were empty. Furthermore, there was one section where the spotless cleanliness of the cavities showed that some utensils had only recently been removed. Six remained, six silver teaspoons . . .

I pushed the drawer closed rapidly and returned to the centre of the room as Mrs Valentine came in. 'The vicar thought he might have left his spectacles here.' We looked quickly round the room but there was no sign of them. I followed her out into the hall and took my leave as she picked up the telephone again. The front door closed behind me and my footsteps crunched across the wet gravel. From what I had seen it seemed almost certain that the teaspoons *had* belonged to Mrs Valentine – also, from the denuded state of the drawer, that other items of cutlery had been removed. Why had Mrs Valentine pretended that nothing was missing? Was she poorly off and getting Mrs Mullins to sell her silver for her? I had noticed no obvious signs of cutting back and it hardly seemed the kind of transaction that she would have confided to Mrs Mullins. It was most peculiar.

I thought about the matter again when I was lying in bed and a more charitable interpretation occurred to me; Mrs

Valentine knew that Mrs Mullins was stealing the silver but was too kind-hearted to say anything about it or inform the police – my intervention had forced her to lie to protect her servant. In terms of loyalty it was a most praiseworthy performance and I wished that I could have found a means of saying so. However, as I had appreciated from Mrs Valentine's reaction, it would not be politic to raise the matter again. I would merely keep a wary eye on the few items of trifling value that I possessed.

I turned over and waited for sleep to come; a few minutes later I turned again. Though not thinking of anything in particular my mind was active and rejecting the idea of sleep. It occurred to me that I was probably worrying about the extra responsibilities I was taking on by becoming secretary to the action committee. I had always been like that; I did not mind doing things but I hated *thinking* about having to do things. I lay on my back and tried to break through into the twilight world, putting my mind into neutral and refusing to let it settle on any specific subject. Against my will, an image began to form as though on a screen coming alive in a darkened cinema. I saw a thick reed bed and a man's head rising above the reeds; he was looking about him anxiously but not moving. As I looked closer I saw that he was unable to move; he was struggling but he remained rooted to the spot. I caught a glimpse of the man's anguished face. It was my own.

A wind was blowing and tracing paths through the reeds, paths that twisted from side to side. As I looked I saw that the paths were converging on the man, then I realized that it was not the wind that was causing the reeds to move. It was something beneath them – some creatures that could not be seen. They were brushing against the reeds as they closed in upon the man. I blinked and shook my head; I wanted the pictures to go away, they were destroying me. I could see my own face clearly; the lips drawn back from the teeth, the expression of terrified apprehension, the stilted movements of the body as it tried to flee. I jerked my own legs and found that they were bound together. I could not break free from this waking nightmare. I closed my eyes tight but I could still see. There was no escape; the dream and the reality were becoming as one. I watched in horror as the man's mouth – my mouth – opened wide to scream; there was no sound. The head suddenly jerked down and hands darted out to fend off some invisible attacker; then the reeds shook and the man disappeared as if being drawn down into some bottomless mire. A dog barked raucously and the image disappeared.

I lay on the bed with the moonlight streaming through the window and sweat dripping from my body. I was cold and terrified but wide awake. I listened intently but there was only the sound of the distant sea. Had I imagined the dog? I waited perhaps five minutes and then went to the window; it was almost like daylight outside and I could see across the marshes. Nothing was moving. In the far distance was a pinpoint of red light which might have been a fishing vessel or a lightship. I patted my pyjamas against my chest to soak up the sweat and pulled on my dressing gown. It was freezing cold yet I had no immediate desire to return to bed; I was frightened that the nightmare would take up where it had left off. I would make myself a cup of tea and read for a bit. One of the good things about retirement, I had told myself, is that you are not tied to a regime; you can work at night and sleep in the day if you want to – in such ways does man rationalize his inability to escape from worldly cares.

I went downstairs and put on the kettle, checking carefully that the water was running clear – this was something that I had not bothered to do for a while and it was depressing to find old fears returning. I made the tea and took myself to the dying embers of the fire, sitting almost in the grate. Normally the wind would have been whistling in the chimney but tonight it was quiet as the grave. For some reason, my glance strayed into a dark corner and there I could make out the white outline of the encyclopedias. I had not looked at them for months and it piqued me that I should suddenly have to be made aware of them now. It reminded me that a bring and buy sale had been mooted as part of the fund-raising activities for the Save Blanely! Association; I decided there and then that the encyclopedias would be my first contribution.

I drained my cup and turned towards the stairs. With a start I saw that there was a light under the door that led down to the jetty; it gave me the eerie impression that there was somebody down there. This was of course impossible but after my recent experience my imagination required no more fuel. I crossed to the light and turned it off. Mrs Mullins must have brushed against it when she was dusting. I was about to go upstairs when I thought I heard something: I froze immediately and there was an unpleasant prickling sensation down my back. From beyond the boathouse door came a faint scratching noise. I hesitated and then turned on the light. I was still not certain whether I had heard or imagined the dog barking; it occurred to me that it was just possible Ripper had been caught in a trap and eventually managed to free himself. Weak and half-starved he might just have had enough strength to struggle back to the boathouse – a dog would have been able to get underneath the grille. I listened again, trying to generate sufficient courage to go down the steps, and just as I had persuaded myself that I had heard nothing and that it was my imagination playing tricks, the noise came again. It was like something scuffling against the downstairs door. I went to the window and looked out.

Down at ground level I could see nothing; everything appeared peaceful. It was cold enough to snow but that was all. I took a deep breath and clapped my hands together, the noise echoing through the house like a pistol shot. I picked up the poker from the grate and crossed to the stairs door. Now that the house was lived in, it did not bind so much and I could pull it open with one hand; I had asked Mrs Mullins's husband to plane a few layers off when he came to do the electrical work but he had done nothing about it. As a workman he had proved satisfactory rather than inspired, a fact that hardly surprised me after my acquaintance with his wife.

I had no intention of prolonging my investigation so I marched heavily down the steps making as much noise as possible, both to boost my spirits and to deter anything that might be lurking on the other side of the door. The cold was intense and seemed to drop a couple of degrees with every step. I arrived at the door and slid back the bolts, catching the sleeve of my dressing gown on one of them; the triple loop of braid that my wife had insisted on sewing to the cuff hooked over the catch. I unsnagged the sleeve and wished that a chance incident had not found this moment to drag my wife's memory before me. I could see her leaning forward with her spectacles slipping down her nose and her needle poised over her knee. I banged my fist against the door, scraping my knuckles. Damn it! I did not wish to send my imagination off down some other dark road. I stood back from the door and pulled it open. The jetty was brightly lit and not only by moonlight – the outside light was on. Before I could stop to puzzle over how this could have happened, something caught my eye: a dark glistening patch on the wall beyond the light. Trickles ran from it, trickles of blood.

At the same instant a half-dead bird tried to drag its broken body inside the house. I slammed the door against it and struck out with the poker, driving it back far enough for me to close the door. There was panic behind my blows, not malice. A small cloud of grey downy feathers settled against my bare ankles and a tiny pinprick line of blood traversed my pyjama trousers. The bird must have been attracted by the light and crashed into the wall; I remembered Mrs Mullins's warning. I found the switch and turned off the light. My heart was pumping furiously and I felt faint. Why in God's name should I be exposed to such physical and mental torture? It was not a question that was difficult to answer.

CHAPTER TEN

It was shortly after the first posters had gone up announcing the inaugural meeting of the Save Blanely! Association that Mrs Valentine received a persuasively worded letter from the Ministry of Power. It stated that the Controller of the Blanely Power Project would be delighted to receive the committee members of the Association and conduct them on a guided tour of the installation under construction. The Minister regretted that 'up until this date, local residents appear to have been less than well-informed' about what was taking place and was certain that the committee members would want to put this matter right by accepting the Controller's invitation; he would of course be delighted to respond to all questions and it was hoped that a frank interchange of views would prevail. Refreshments would be provided.

Colonel Fraser was quick to note that the address given for a reply was not at the Ministry of Power but to a firm in New Bond Street called MediaMessage.

'They're trying to smarm us off with a bunch of smart-alec public relations men,' was his comment. 'Having tried to pull the wool over our eyes they're now bringing out the soft soap.'

'I don't see how we can refuse the invitation though,' said Doctor Parr. 'We must arm ourselves with the facts. In this way we're going to be better equipped when it comes to action.'

'Yes, I think we must go,' said Mrs Valentine thoughtfully. 'I agree with Doctor Parr – though, of course, accepting the Colonel's advice that we should be on our mettle. What do you think, vicar?' The vicar thought that he ought not to go because it might put the Church in an invidious position and he was certain that the bishop might not like it; he quoted the controversy that had been created by the participation of certain clerics in the Aldermaston marches, protesting against the hydrogen bomb. When asked by the Colonel what the bishop's reaction had been to the question of a special collection for the fighting fund, the vicar said that he had not yet found a propitious moment to raise the subject. This reply was once again sufficient to ensure that the vicar was banished beyond the outer perimeters of the Colonel's vision for the rest of the meeting.

I remember the day selected for the visit well, because it coincided with the first snow of the winter. Five of us – Colonel Fraser, Mrs Valentine, Doctor Parr, a determined spinster lady from the other end of the village called Mrs Murchison, who was a substitute for the vicar, and myself – all squeezed into the Colonel's Range Rover. This was ostensibly a measure against the elements but I think we all felt happier arriving in a phalanx having exchanged a quarter of an hour's small talk. I was now at a stage when I found myself revelling in the company of others. Since the incident with the bird I had a horror of being alone at night and a terrible sense of foreboding; I was frightened of going to sleep in case I started dreaming yet found lying awake and listening to every sound almost as alarming. A fertile imagination and a bad conscience can create a whole nightmarish world with the pattern of moonlight through a curtain. One of the things that disturbed me most about the injured bird was that there had been no sign of it in the morning. I could have understood this had the tide been in, but the creek was almost empty and anything that had flopped into it would have been visible. I tried to persuade myself that a cat or even a fox had carried it off but it was not easy.

Much of our talk on the way to the site centred on what kind of man the 'Controller' would be. I think we all saw him as some kind of insensitive boffin blinking at us from behind rimless spectacles; we felt pretty certain that he would wear a white coat and spout incomprehensible jargon. The reality was totally different. A frank-faced, middle-aged man with a moustache that was almost rakish and a cultivated voice, he wore a lightweight overcoat from the bottom of which protruded the trousers of a country suit.

Mr Brownly, for that was his name, was waiting for us at the main entrance to the site which was marked by a weighted white pole that swung down across the road. It was like the entrance to an army camp; two security men sat behind the window of a prefabricated shed and there was another wary-eyed alsatian in attendance. The security men did not move and it was Mr Brownly who bent down to greet us and point out where the car should be parked. He walked along behind us and was joined by another man whom he introduced as his assistant; he looked like a younger version of the Controller and was, at a guess, not long down from university.

It was difficult to take a dislike to these men on first acquaintance; their manner was civilized and friendly, almost deferential, and we were made to feel that we had performed a service by putting in an appearance. After some ice-breaking badinage on the inclemency of the weather, the Controller led the way through the falling snow towards the circular concrete shape with the kiln in the middle. I noticed him lean forward and glance at the Colonel's tie as if confirming something. 'Thirteen-eighteenth? You must have seen quite a lot of service in Germany.' He mentioned his own regiment and soon he and the Colonel were joined in a conversation that was almost animated; I could see that the Colonel's pre-determined attitude of suspicion bordering on antipathy was already being undermined.

The snow was settling and we were like crumbs on a vast white tablecloth that had been cleared of everything save the structure before us. We walked through wide Norman arches and the pursuing snow melted away into wet, dark stains. It seemed even colder than in the open. I heard the sound of sea hissing against shingle and, as we came round the corner of some enormous buttresses, was surprised to see that the marsh had now been scooped away so that the sea actually came in amongst the piles of the building. The shingle must have been brought in by the fleet of lorries that even now were symbolically churning up the snow into ugly black caterpillar tracks.

'I must say,' said Mrs Valentine firmly, 'that I am most surprised, not to say astonished, that work has proceeded as far as this without the local residents being given a true idea of what is happening.'

The Controller's reply was disarmingly frank. 'So am I,' he said. 'I'm afraid it was a state of affairs that was allowed to develop before I became involved with the project. As soon as I realized that there was a whole area of confusion and uncertainty I took immediate steps to try and put things right. That is, of course, why you have all been invited here today.'

It was clear that this reply had a chastening effect on all present. One could hardly blame Mr Brownly for something that was not his fault and which he was trying to put right.

'I don't see why we have to have the thing here at all,' said the Colonel almost apologetically. 'Couldn't you have put it up the north end of Scotland?'

'Well, we *have* put them up the north end of Scotland,' said the Controller pleasantly. 'In fact we've put them everywhere. We do try and spread them about. If I may say so, I think that behind your question lurks a belief that nuclear reactors are dangerous. Now, in fact, nothing could be further from the truth. A number of scare stories have appeared in the press which have been far too easily accepted by the public. I'm certain you would agree that the press can often inflame situations in a way that is little short of scandalous.' Doctor Parr nodded in sympathy with the last statement; he had said as much himself. 'If we were talking about a conventional power station then I don't think anybody would experience a twinge of alarm. I mean, you don't feel alarmed when you drive past a gasometer, do you?'

'Only by its ugliness,' said Mrs Valentine disapprovingly.

Mr Brownly stopped as if on a cue and waved his arm about him. I had the impression that he had carefully fed in the reference to the gasometer in order to encourage just the reaction he had received. 'And that's another point in favour of this particular reactor: it is not a monstrous structure towering into the sky with chimneys and all that kind of thing. Most of the working gubbins is below ground level; it keeps a very low profile. I'll show you some artists' drawings of the finished article in a few moments.' He led the way towards a ramp that sloped underground. 'As your own experience will have shown you, anything looks at its worst when it's being built, especially in winter. The final appearance of this place will be like a mushroom.'

'A mushroom cloud,' I said. I don't know why I spoke the words out loud; the image just popped into my mind and then out of my mouth. The Colonel glared at me and the Controller's composure was ruffled for the first time. He smiled uneasily, as if not sure whether I was trying to be critical or make a joke.

'You used the words "this particular reactor",' said Mrs Valentine, coming to the rescue. 'Does this mean that there is something unusual about it?'

'Very perceptive.' Mr Brownly congratulated Mrs Valentine with a smile. 'I was just coming to that.' We were now in an underground chamber that reminded me of a giant boiler room; it was almost as warm, too – a marked contrast to the temperature outside. I was amazed to find that so much had been completed. The men who were walking about looked more like technicians than workmen; I saw one examining a gauge and making a note on a pad.

'Is this thing operational?' said the Colonel, incredulous.

'This is the marvel of this new kind of reactor,' said the Controller. 'As you probably know, or as you may not know, a conventional nuclear reactor takes years to build. As you certainly do know, the country's fuel needs are immediate. British scientists have found a way of processing uranium in a much simpler and more direct way, and the whole procedure has now been streamlined. I think it's something that we as a nation can feel justifiably proud of.' He looked at us searchingly, as if challenging anybody to be unpatriotic enough to disagree.

'So this is going to be the first of its kind?' I asked.

'On this scale, yes,' said the Controller. 'Of course, there have been working models. The whole thing is a tried and tested concept.'

'Why did you have to choose to put it here?' said Mrs Valentine. There was a note of crushed resignation in her voice as if she realized that the battle was already lost.

'Water,' said the Controller. 'We need lots of water to cool the turbine – and I'm certain you'll agree that there's nothing much cooler than the North Sea at this time of year.' His small joke produced no more than a courteous smile.

'The turbine is behind those doors, is it?' asked the Colonel. He indicated some heavy metal doors that reminded me of the bulkhead of a ship. As we looked at them, one opened and we could see that they were double doors with a small area between; the second door was closed. The man who emerged was covered from head to foot in a uniform like a space suit, his features invisible behind helmet and visor. He wore heavy protective gloves and carried a covered steel basket containing five bottle-like phials. His sudden appearance was unsettling and a momentary expression of annoyance passed across the Controller's face; he glanced at his watch and turned away from the doors. 'Yes, that's the turbine house. I'd be delighted to show it to you but technically I don't think it would mean a great deal. There's also that piece of paper called the Official Secrets Act.' He pretended to scrutinize us. 'I don't think any of you look like Russian spies but one can never be too careful.'

I looked back towards the men in the protective clothing. He was laboriously opening another door by moving steel levers. 'Presumably there's a risk as well,' I said.

'Radiation,' said Mrs Murchison, opening her mouth for the first time since we had arrived.

The Controller was trying to lead the way towards a half open door beyond which I could see a table laid out with glasses. He stopped and turned to face us. 'There are codes of safety practice laid down in any responsible organization,' he said. 'I think we should beware of employing emotive phrases which have been bandied about by the press until they are meaningless.' He sounded hurt, as if his confidence in the ultimate good of human nature had been shaken. He gestured about him. 'I think that, one day, what is being achieved here will astound the world. We may envy the Americans their space programme, but in the long term what our British scientists have achieved may be of more benefit to humanity. What is ultimately more important, ladies and gentlemen, the conquest of space or the conquest of those problems that face us here on Earth?' A silence greeted these remarks during which I looked round for the man in the protective clothing. He had disappeared but his image stayed in my mind. 'I sincerely believe that to have had its name associated with this project may, one day, make Blanely proud.' There was no voice for or against, and the Controller gestured towards the open door. 'And now, in rather frugal surroundings I must confess, we would like to offer you something to keep the cold at bay. We can also have a look at those drawings I was talking about.' We moved forward dutifully like sheep towards a dip. Even the Colonel was reduced to fingering his tie. 'If you *are* going to hold a meeting,' said the Controller innocently, 'I would be most delighted to come along and tell everybody what we're up to.'

Soon we all had glasses in our hands and the Controller's assistant was passing round illustrations of what the reactor would look like when it was finished. It did resemble a mushroom, one with a short stem, lying upside down on a cromlech of concrete piles. The artist had painted in wispy trees nearby which bore no resemblance to the real-life situation and for this the Controller apologized.

I think we had all taken rather a knock and were wonder-

ing where we could possibly go from here; I was glad that it
was Colonel Fraser and Mrs Valentine who had to take the
responsibility for decision making. I detached myself from
the group and went up and outside into the open area. It was
still snowing and a north wind was blowing the snow almost
horizontally through the arches; occasional flakes would sting
my face. I turned up my collar and dug my hands deep into
my pockets. The lorries had ground to a halt and nobody
seemed to be working. The windscreen of the Colonel's car
was covered by a layer of snow. I walked out along one of the
groynes watching the sea beneath me, which seemed to be
going through some kind of gate; it made a honking, snorting
noise like a man trying to clear his throat. I suddenly thought
of my wife in the sluice.

'Careful how you go. It's rather slippery underfoot.' The
Controller had arrived at my shoulder without my hearing
him. My heart jumped again and a flurry of snow made me
duck away and turn my back against the wind. The sea slapped
against the groyne.

'What about the worms?' I said. The Controller searched
my face as if for some small clue which would make the meaning of my words transparently clear. There was no trace of
apprehension or censure in his eyes. If I do not understand,
said his frank, level gaze, then the fault is totally on my side.
'They've disappeared.'

The Controller nodded as if meaning was beginning to per-
colate. 'If you're worried about the balance of nature and that
kind of thing, you need have no qualms.' A thought struck
him. 'In fact a nuclear reactor has been known to have a very
salutary effect. Saviour of the Colchester oyster ... Warm
water pumped out from our Bradwell reactor resuscitated a
dying breed – they thrived on it. Waxed fat and juicy.' I looked
down to where the snowflakes were flecking the restless surface of the dark water like spent bullets. 'We just use the sea for
cooling the turbine. There's no damage to the environment',
he went on. I started to think of oysters waxing fat and juicy;

somehow, the words used conjured up images that alarmed me. I looked through the snow and saw the Colonel and the rest of them waiting under the shelter of the main structure. I felt an overwhelming desire to get away from this gaunt intimation of the future and from the persuasive Controller.

'I think they're waiting,' I said and started to walk back towards the groyne.

'If I can send you any literature . . .' said the Controller.

'What happened to you?' the Colonel asked huffily, but he was not interested in a reply; he just wanted to make it clear that he disapproved of me wandering off, undermining his leadership.

'I'm sorry,' I said. 'I found it a bit stuffy down there.'

'I'm so glad you could come,' said the Controller. 'I hope you've got a much better idea of what it's all about. Doubtless we'll be in touch with each other.' He made no move to step out from under the awning and see us to the Range Rover.

The Colonel stuck out a hand. 'Thank you. Most interesting.'

We said various kinds of goodbyes and stumbled out into the snow. I don't think that one of us said another word until we were nearly back at Marsh House.

CHAPTER ELEVEN

No more posters announcing the inaugural meeting of the Save Blanely! Association were put up after our visit to the reactor and in fact I had the impression that some of those already up were discreetly taken down. There was even what Mrs Valentine called 'an atmosphere' when the Vicar came down off his fence and announced the meeting when he read out the parish notices during the Sunday service. The unfortunate man could not understand why this gesture apparently did not improve his relations with the Colonel.

The meeting when it occurred was a low-key affair. The attendance was poor because of the bad weather conditions and competition from television, and if there were any newspaper reporters present I did not see them. The local M.P. certainly did not put in an appearance. Colonel Fraser was in the chair but his was no fire-and-brimstone address such as one might have expected from his initial vehement opposition to the reactor. He made a statement of the situation and described our tour of the site, repeating many of the arguments advanced by the Controller. Although Mr Brownly's offer to address the meeting had not been taken up, there was a pile of literature available that he had sent, and Mrs Murchison announced that the Women's Institute had been invited to visit the site with the promise of light refreshments – the Young Farmers' Club, too. It was significant that, when the time came for questions, the only two that were asked related to the possibility of the reactor providing jobs for local people, and it was doubtless no coincidence that the edition of the local paper which came out after the meeting carried an article by Mr Brownly saying how the new reactor would certainly create employment in the area. The meeting was covered in a few lines under the anodyne headline 'Blanely villagers gather to hear about new reactor'. There was no doubt in my mind but that the Controller was aptly named, and that any teeth the Save Blanely! Association might have once possessed had been drawn as if from an old dog. Whist drives, house-to-house collections, bring and buy sales and other fund-raising activities were not even mentioned and I recall reflecting that the dreaded encyclopedias would probably gather dust on my shelves for another few months unless I went to the length of throwing them away.

All this time I was becoming increasingly nervous and apprehensive; the optimism of the previous May had completely disappeared. With the virtual acceptance of the nuclear reactor it was as if a black shadow had fallen across the land, one that would never go away. It is difficult for me to explain my feelings exactly because I always saw it as representing evil in a way that defied analysis. I had known for a long time that something was building up, something frightening and terrible, and now I felt I was actually in the presence of its catalyst. Just out of my sight but never out of my mind was the dark, brooding mass disturbing the already troubled balance of nature.

I slept badly and was troubled by such hideous dreams that daylight came as a blessed relief. More and more often I was tortured by visions of my wife and of Wilson; her bloated whiteness would extend a swollen, accusing arm towards me; Wilson's heart would be pumping like a balloon as the dying fish jumped about his body. Always, always, there were worms – emerging from every orifice: nose, ears, mouth, rectum, singly and in unending streams, always writhing obscenely. Sometimes these worms would give birth to other worms extruding from their bodies like excrement until my whole imagination was full to bursting and I would explode into sweat-soaked wakefulness. Of course my feelings of guilt were induced by fear but they were no less genuine for that; no pain that my wife had caused me was like the torment I was undergoing now. I was being pursued by small writhing demons and what was so terrifying was that as their mental presence increased so their physical presence diminished – I never saw a worm these days. It worried me so much that I even began to look for them. I would pull back stones, terrified but still hoping to catch a glimpse of a small red shape sliding beneath the earth. I was almost disappointed. I watched the thrushes and the blackbirds on the Marsh House lawn; their heads would be cocked expectantly but I never saw one with a worm. The banks of the dykes that I had seen pock-marked with casts were now smooth. Where *were* the worms? Had some blight wiped them out? I thought not; I had the strange and terrifying premonition that they were indeed there, somewhere, waiting for something. Sometimes in the small hours I would lie awake and think of the list of worms that I had read in the encyclopedia; their nauseatingly evocative names would be typed out neatly on the white paper of the ceiling. I would imagine them, massed, united, boring through my body like white hot wire.

Why, you may ask, did I stay in this place with its increasingly morbid and apocalyptic associations? Why does an alcoholic continue to reach for the bottle or a heroin addict the syringe? Those in the grip of death have no free will; they are programmed to their environment as I was to this desolate marshland. I could not escape from it. At my most sanguine all I could believe was that I had sinned and that I must wait for whatever punishment was coming to me.

All I did wish was that I could talk to somebody – confide my fears. I envied the Catholic his confessional, but how could I tell a part without telling all? Could I describe the worms without revealing why they persecuted me? Because I had killed two people. With every day that went by the need to unburden myself became greater and it was perhaps this that caused me to pause one morning as I walked past the church. The vicar's bicycle leant against the porch and I hesitated only a moment before entering the graveyard. As I did so, he emerged carrying in his arms a large bunch of withered holly.

I was reminded of when I had first met him; again, one of those moments of *déjà vu* that seemed to be happening with unnerving frequency.

We exchanged greetings and the vicar shook his head as he followed the path round the side of the church. 'This holly has been in the church since Christmas. It really is too bad. Berries all over the transept. I'll have to speak to Mrs Murchison; her ladies are supposed to be responsible for the flowers.'

I sympathized and watched as he threw the holly onto what had become a compost heap of grass cuttings and dead flowers from the graves. Snow still covered the ground and it was obvious that nothing had been added to the heap since the snow had fallen. 'Look at that!' The vicar clucked and advanced to a grave that had an elaborate posy of plastic flowers on it.

'How many times do I have to make my feelings clear on that point. I will not have those abominations in my graveyard. That's that Hargreaves woman. I'm not surprised.'

Again I sympathized and wondered if there was any point in trying to approach my dilemma. If the vicar was agitated by the sight of plastic flowers on a grave, I scarcely dared think about his reaction to my crimes. A sense of desperation began to grip me.

'How odd.' The vicar had seen something else. I moved to his side and followed his puzzled gaze. By the yew hedge in the corner of the graveyard was a grave that was completely free of snow. It lay there, a neat, grass-covered rectangle. There were no footprints in the snow around it and no indication that it had been swept.

'How very strange,' I said, and together we approached the grave. The grass was gleaming, the earth beneath it black and moist. On an impulse I bent down and touched the ground. I withdrew my hand quickly: the earth was warm. Furthermore it gave off a faint but discernible vibration. The vicar saw my reaction and looked at me questioningly.

'It feels warm,' I said. 'Perhaps there's a drainage pipe or something like that running beneath the graveyard.'

He raised his eyes beyond the yew hedge to an uncultivated orchard being strangled with ivy. Behind the other corner of the graveyard was a ploughed field lying beneath a coverlet of snow. 'Possibly,' he said without conviction.

The silence began to weigh on me. 'Whose grave was it?'

'William Wilson's.' I stepped back as if from a suddenly revealed snake pit. A throbbing bolt of terror passed through my heart. Although I had attended the service I had not participated at the interment; if I imagine the sound of a shovelful of earth hitting the top of a coffin I become nauseous.

The Vicar read the consternation in my face although he clearly did not understand all the reasons for it. He plucked at my sleeve and began to walk back towards the church. I followed, still feeling the movement of the ground vibrating through my fingertips.

'There is much that is strange about this place,' he said, almost to himself. 'I never feel, how can I put it, at ease here.'

'I know exactly what you mean,' I said, finding it easy to agree with him.

He paused in the porch and shivered. 'I sometimes think it must be the coldest church in England.' He paused. 'I know I should not say so, but I wonder if in part it does not come from the people who worship in it.' The inner door was now swung open and he looked down the nave towards the two stone effigies lying with hands folded in prayer. 'It is a tradition that goes back a long way.' I said nothing but followed him towards the tombs. It was true that the cold was almost insupportable; it seemed to enter into your bones. In this glacial atmosphere the rectangle of warm earth outside was even more bizarre, more sinister. I avoided looking at the swaying worms on the side of the tombs.

'Sir Robert de Wicklem.' The vicar looked down at the pious stone face and pronounced the name like that of a criminal awaiting sentence. 'Perhaps it all began with you.' He turned to me and indicated the effigies. 'These two were apparently not as devoted to each other as their proximity in death suggests. I have made local history one of my pursuits and there are some interesting chronicles of the time, what one might describe as gossipy letters to a friend in Norwich by a spinster neighbour of the de Wicklems. She reports that Sir Robert de Wicklem treated his wife shamefully, beating her and deceiving her with any local wench who took his fancy. There are details of this side of the relationship that it distresses me to think about, let alone repeat. He was far from reticent in the conduct of his affairs.' The vicar's gaze which had strayed to Lady de Wicklem, quickly moved to the altar cross. 'The poor woman was eventually found dead in a ditch near the house. She had been struck about the head and de Wicklem maintained that she had been murdered by foot-pads, whilst taking alms to the church. He claimed she had been carrying several pieces of silver, which were never found. Of course, there were many local people who disagreed with this version of the truth and said that de Wicklem had killed his wife in a drunken rage. Nevertheless, he was the lord of the manor and his word was upheld. According to the letters, a local simpleton was arrested for the crime and eventually hung, drawn and quartered.'

I looked down at the demurely closed eyes and the aristo-cratic nose and high cheekbones. Now that I examined the face carefully there was a cruel quality about the small, almost lipless mouth and the severe lines that ran down to the trian-gular spade beard. In some inexplicable way the face vaguely reminded me of someone, though I could not decide who.

'So he got away with it,' I said.

The vicar hesitated. 'Well, we don't know. It can never be definitely proved whether he was innocent or guilty. The inter-esting fact is that he died the day after the execution of the man held responsible for the crime. He went out riding and his horse came back from the marshes without him. His body was never found.'

'Perhaps somebody took revenge,' I suggested.

'Perhaps.' He turned away, his brows knitted thoughtfully.

'It is a strange story is it not? I know it is a tenet of the Christian faith that people should be forgiven their sins but I cannot help feeling that the presence of this man pollutes the atmosphere of the church. He does not belong here and yet his effigy presides over our worship.'

I avoided the vicar's eyes. Little did he realize that he was addressing a man perhaps as infamous before God as was Robert de Wicklem. How could I bring myself to confess to him? He would have no compassion for me. Thin shafts of winter sunshine broke through the windows in the south wall and motes hung in the air. The shadow of Sir Robert's tomb was twisted and thrown, against a line of memorial plaques and embossed urns. It was strange, but the shape was almost like a pointing finger indicating one particular brass plate that stood out from the others. I crossed to read the plate: *In loving memory of Edgar George Henry Valentine, departed this life February 16, 1955.*

'Mrs Valentine's husband?' I asked. The vicar nodded. 'And where is he buried?'

He frowned and looked surprised. 'Surely you know?'

'I haven't made a detailed examination of the graveyard,' I said. 'Is there a family plot?'

'The late Mr Valentine died in a boating accident. His body was never recovered.'

'Good heavens.' This small blasphemy was the last thing to escape my lips for several seconds. The information stunned me; I had never thought to inquire about the cause of Mr Valentine's death.

'I'm amazed that you did not know,' said the vicar. 'I suppose in the terrible circumstances of your own wife's death, Mrs Valentine thought it best to avoid the subject. She has a great deal of sensibility.'

'And reserve,' I said. 'I think that must have something to do with it. Poor woman. She has hardly mentioned her husband to me, apart from saying that he used to use my cottage as a workshop.' I suddenly saw her standing before the portrait in the drawing room on the night when I had peered through the curtains. 'It is his portrait that hangs above the fireplace?'

He nodded. 'Yes. I never met the man; he died a few years before I came to the parish. I only heard about him.' He looked as if he was going to say more and then checked himself.

An impulse made me glance at the side of the tomb. The sunlight played upon the worms and their tiny shadows seemed to be following the line of the pointing finger towards the brass memorial plaque. Then the sunlight disappeared and the images vanished. The church was dark, gloomy and very, very cold.

I started to move towards the door. 'I'm glad you told me about Mr Valentine,' I said. 'I must choose my moment and mention the subject to Mrs Valentine. She probably thinks it strange that I have never said anything.'

'She probably thinks that you are being discreet.'

'Probably.'

We were now in the porch and I extended a hand. 'Well, I must be on my way. I'll see you on Sunday, no doubt.'

'Vespers,' reminded the vicar. He took my hand and immediately released it. 'Your hand! It's like ice.'

I felt my hand and then touched my face. I could feel nothing.

He was looking at me incredulously.

'I'm very cold-blooded,' I said.

I started to walk down the path to the lych gate and the marsh. I could sense his eyes following me but I did not turn round.

CHAPTER TWELVE

When I got back to my cottage I was surprised to find that the key was not hidden in its normal place. It was one of Betty Mullins's afternoons and it was agreed between us that I would leave the front door key propped in the corner of a window sill if I went out; she would lock up and replace the key when she went home.

I tried the front door and it was open; immediately, I felt a sense of foreboding. I paused in the doorway and called Mrs Mullins's name. There was no reply. I looked across the room and could see the key lying beside the sink; I retrieved it and returned it to the lock. A dustpan and brush were lying on the floor at the foot of the stairs. I called out again: no answer. A thin trickle of sweat was running down my back, icy cold. I took a deep breath and started up the stairs. Very slowly, I raised my head above floor level. I was staring at a carpet-sweeper; my bed was unmade, and there was no sign of Mrs Mullins. Not for the first time, I had the feeling that I was going mad; the gap between reality and my nightmares had disappeared. I thought of Mrs Valentine's missing dog, the vanishing of the worms, the maimed bird on the jetty . . .

The windows rattled and a door banged. My heart jumped. It must have been the door at the bottom of the boathouse steps. Perhaps Mrs Mullins had slipped and injured herself. In a state of mounting fear I went down the stairs and pulled open the top door; a shaft of light at the bottom revealed that the door to the jetty was open. It banged again ominously. I shouted Mrs Mullins's name; a piece of sedge blew through the door and all I could hear was the wind. I started down the stairs, my heart pounding. The door slammed behind me and I cried out in panic. It was cold but I felt nothing, only fear. I reached the bottom and braced myself to look out; I pushed my head round the door jamb. The jetty was empty. I went forward and braced myself to look in the dyke. The tide was out. Something moved in the few inches of brackish water at the bottom and I opened my mouth to scream, but it was only a small crab burying itself in the mud; it disappeared as into a fog. Trembling, I returned to the stairs and bolted the door behind me. I had not put the light on so I was now in darkness; it was like being in a tomb. I ran up the stairs and thrust open the door, relieved to be in what remained of the daylight again.

Then I really screamed.

Dangling over the side of the armchair was a human hand. Conquering the impulse to run from the room, I stepped forward and found Mrs Mullins slumped in the high-backed armchair which was pushed forward close to the fire; she must have been there all the time. Her face was grey, with beads of sweat at the temples and on the upper lip and for a moment I thought that she was dead. Then it struck me that she had probably had a stroke. Frightened to touch her with my bare hand, I fetched a bowl of water from the sink and began to dab her face with a wet tissue. She suddenly groaned and her eyes opened; her hands moved to her stomach and her mouth gaped like a dying fish. She seemed to be in great pain and I felt powerless, like a bystander at a bad car crash. I emptied the bowl and placed it on her lap. She was clearly trying to be sick; she twitched and the bowl fell to the floor. A rime of froth began to form at the corners of her mouth. I hesitated and then ran from the room. I had to get help.

It had started to thaw and water was dripping from the roof and trees as I ran towards Marsh House. Patches of the drive were already clear and there was a large puddle before the front door step. I rang the bell and banged on the knocker, listening to the noise echoing through the house. Mrs Mullins had been looking worse lately but I had never expected it to come to this: I heard footsteps approaching and Mrs Valentine opened the door. My distress must have been evident.

'What is it?' she asked, staring.

'It's Mrs Mullins—'

Immediately, her face registered alarm. I remember thinking at the time that she seemed to have been expecting something to happen. 'What's the matter?'

'I came back from a walk and found that she'd collapsed while she was doing the housework. I think she may be dying.'

'I'll come at once.' Mrs Valentine started after me and then hesitated. 'You go back. I'll get some things and follow you.' She disappeared into the house and I started to run back down the path. Now it was raining, a thin drizzle mixed with sleet; the temperature had dropped dramatically. When I got back to the cottage, Mrs Mullins was slumped over the side of the chair, a thin trail of vomit dribbling from her mouth to the floor. This time I thought she must be dead, but as I turned on the light she made a wheezing noise at the back of her throat. Memories began to stir through my immediate panic, and Mrs Valentine's arrival was not a moment too soon. She carried a tray of bottles into the kitchen, returned and swiftly pulled Mrs Mullins into an upright position. I was surprised how physically strong and assertive she could be when it was necessary.

'Bring me the bottle from the sink and a tablespoon.'

There were three bottles. 'Which one?'

'It's got a green sticker on the bottom.'

I examined each of the bottles. 'I can't see a sticker.'

She turned and indicated a bottle. 'That one. Pour out a tablespoonful and give it to her while I hold her mouth open.'

She grasped Mrs Mullins's head whilst I prepared the dose. The spoon was poised when Mrs Mullins opened her eyes and started to struggle furiously.

'Give it to her! Hurry up!'

Mrs Mullins choked on her false teeth and I took the chance to push the spoon into her mouth. It was horribly like dosing an animal. Some of the liquid ran down her chin and she tried to spit the rest against my chest. I pushed the spoon to the very back of her throat and forced her to swallow. I could not understand why she was reacting so violently.

'Surely she needs a doctor,' I gasped.

'Of course – when she's had her medicine. We'll take her to the house and ring for Doctor Parr.' Mrs Mullins uttered a cry of pain and fell back against the chair; she appeared to have sunk into a coma. Mrs Valentine immediately seized her arm and started to try and pull her to her feet. Distressed and thoroughly confused, I moved to help her. 'She'll be warmer in my house. I've got plenty of blankets.' Her voice was urgent.

I said nothing but draped Mrs Mullins's inert arm over my shoulder. I was far from loath to remove her from my own house; I have never reacted well to the presence of sick people and I much preferred that the responsibility and vicarious suffering be fairly and squarely in Mrs Valentine's domain. I felt incapable of coping. Together we half carried, half dragged Mrs Mullins back to Marsh House and placed her in front of the drawing room fire. She lay there like a sacrificial offering with rain and sweat gleaming on her face. Above the fireplace, illuminated by the dancing flames, Mr Valentine presided over the scene.

Mrs Valentine fetched blankets and placed a pillow beneath Mrs Mullins's head. 'Watch her,' she said. 'I'll telephone for Doctor Parr.' She came back in two minutes, looking puzzled.

'He's not there. I talked to his housekeeper. Apparently he was called to the reactor yesterday and there's been no word from him since.'

I felt an immediate pang of fear and premonition. 'Do you think something's gone wrong?'

'We mustn't be alarmist.' Mrs Valentine frowned as if remembering something. 'It is curious though. Mrs Murchison rang me up this afternoon. She was most put out because the Women's Institute visit to the reactor was cancelled at the last moment without any explanation.'

A log exploded in the grate and Mrs Mullins groaned as if

alarmed by the noise. I felt that the noose was tightening. 'Can you ring the reactor and tell Doctor Parr what's happened?'

Mrs Valentine considered and nodded. 'Very well.' She went out and I heard her dialling. My eyes strayed round the room, eager to avoid looking at the bundle by the fireplace, and lit upon the sideboard; suddenly I remembered the strange saga of the missing spoons. Not for the first time I had the feeling that something was going on that I had only just begun to penetrate. Against my will I glanced at Mrs Mullins; her head was tilted to one side and her mouth was slightly open, and as I watched she began to gulp like a stranded fish. I thought of my drowned wife, but pushed the memory away. My eyes went to the portrait. The stern, unbending face of Mr Valentine now looked uncommonly as if it was smiling.

'I can't get through.' Mrs Valentine's voice made me jump. 'It's making a number unobtainable noise.'

'Something must have gone wrong,' I said. 'Badly wrong. We'll have to dial 999. And then there's her husband – he must be wondering what's happened.'

'They're not on the telephone.' Her voice was distant, and I noticed her fingers were plucking at each other uneasily. Half a dozen thoughts and fears were no doubt running through her mind. Mrs Mullins groaned again.

'We must do something,' I said. 'I'll ring if you like.' I did not wait for an answer but went into the hall and picked up the telephone. The line was dead. I pounded the rest and listened again. The silence seemed to have an almost tangible quality. She was watching from the doorway. 'The line's gone dead,' I said.

'It's incredible. What can be happening?'

'I'm frightened to think,' I said, and looked towards the drawing room. 'We'll have to take her to hospital.'

Mrs Valentine shook her head vehemently. 'No. I don't think we should move her again.'

'What can we do then?'

'There's a cottage hospital at Boston Market. You could

drive there and get a doctor.' She saw that I was hesitating and pulled open the drawer of the table on which the telephone rested. 'I'll show you the map.' She unfolded the map and her finger moved quickly to the spot. 'It's only about six miles away.' She looked up at me. 'Or you could try and find Doctor Parr at the reactor.'

'I don't know what to do.' I was terrified of leaving the house, terrified of staying in it. I was also confused – too many things were happening, too many decisions had to be made. I was no longer capable of stepping outside my predicament and examining it objectively. I was being carried along by the tide of events.

'Try the cottage hospital.' Mrs Valentine had taken my arm and was guiding me towards the front door. 'I'll stay here and do what I can. Maybe the telephone will come on again. Good luck.'

The door closed behind me and I was alone. It was dark and the rain spattered against my face. Dutifully I felt in my pocket for the key; it was not there – it must be in the house. The snow was melting fast and turning to slush. It was almost warm now, or perhaps it was me; maybe I was becoming feverish. I felt tired and ill. My nerves were on edge. About me, every shadow seemed to hide a demon. I looked at the cottage; the lights had been left on, four yellow squares against the darkness. Once I had wanted that house more than anything else in the world; now I hated it with a loathing born of fear. I had killed for it and now it was destroying me. Glowing with light, it made me feel that there was somebody else there, a sensation I often had when I returned. I was never alone. There was always other invisible presences. I threw open the door and felt my stomach contract as I looked towards the armchair; I had a terrible premonition that there was going to be someone in it, but it was empty.

I went upstairs and took the car keys from the bedside table. On an impulse I crossed to the window and looked out; I could see nothing. There was no moon, no distant lights from the sea. My eyes probed the darkness in the direction of the reactor, but I could not see even the usual few twinkling lights.

A sound reached my ears. I paused; first I thought it was the wind, a very faint rustling, almost imperceptible. I hesitated and opened the window. I felt cold air against my face but there was not a breath of wind, and the rain had stopped. The noise was unlike any I had ever heard before: a scraping, sliding, slithery note that might have been made with a violin bow and a too-tight string, but there was no music in it, only menace.

I closed the window and shut the catch firmly. My nerves must be playing me tricks; I had read of overwrought people hearing strange noises, singing in the ears ... I almost ran down the stairs and locked the front door behind me, leaving on all the lights. My car was in the drive in front of the house and Mrs Valentine watched from the drawing-room window as I hurried past. The curtain fell back into place as I climbed into the car. I fumbled the key into the ignition and found that I did not have the map with me; on reflection I could not remember whether Mrs Valentine had given it to me but it did not matter too much. I knew where Boston Market was, and I could ask for the hospital when I got there. I checked that there was enough petrol in the car and started down the drive. Water was dripping from the overhanging laurels and I switched on the windscreen wipers; the drive was like a tunnel. The headlights picked out the gateposts and as I slowed down and pulled out into the road, the windscreen wipers started to squeak against the dry glass; I turned them off. Ahead the road ran straight for nearly a mile with the marsh on the seaward side. I was heading towards the reactor but due to turn off inland before I got there. Suddenly I saw something glistening in the road.

At first I thought it was flood water flowing out from the marches. I stamped on the brakes and then saw to my horror that the swelling tide was not water – it was worms, millions of them. They were emerging from the reeds so fast that layers of them were building on top of each other like fish being tipped from a barrel. As I watched, almost paralysed with terror, a crawling, slithering mass spilled towards me; I panicked and accelerated towards them. The tyres slapped into the first wave and almost immediately the windscreen was obliterated by a moving screen of worms. Blinded, I switched on the windscreen wipers and braked sharply. It was as if I had run into a patch of black ice; the crushed worms turned to slippery slime, which provoked a violent skid that ended with my head smashing against the windscreen and the car slewing into a ditch.

I felt blood trickling down my forehead and desperately tried to restart the engine; it roared to life but when I engaged a gear the back wheels merely threw mud down the road. Mud and worms. One headlight played down the ditch and all I could see was a wriggling mass of worms, building up layer upon layer with every fresh wave that wriggled across the road. They were not unduly large; what was so terrifying was the sheer weight of numbers in which they continued to pour from the marshes. All the time that there had been no sight of a worm they must have been massing in their millions. I looked down the writhing ditch and felt as though I was in the intestinal tract of an infested animal. It was back to Hieronymus Bosch; I was part of the hideous painting in the solicitor's waiting room.

As I stared out of my prison I was seized by a new fear: the worms were changing direction and coming towards the car. They spilled slowly towards me like oily waves. Were the headlights attracting them? I turned off the lights and shivered in the darkness. I could hear the noise of them moving, the noise I had heard from the cottage window: the terrible squeaking of their slippery bodies elongating and contracting across each other. I could see the dark shadow of the night sky through the windscreen but this slowly began to disappear as if a ragged curtain was being pulled across the glass. Unable to stand not seeing anything any longer, I turned on the light in the car. I looked about me and screamed. The outside of every window in the car was now covered in a thick layer of worms; their bodies showed pink as they pressed against the glass and they weaved and interlaced like raffia matting, shutting out any other view. The feeling of terror and claustrophobia was paralysing. I was entombed. What was even more horrifying was the fact that they were obviously trying to get inside the car, I could see them bunching and straining around the door edges. Desperately I turned my head from side to side and closed the windows more firmly.

It was then that I felt something cold and slimy touch my ankle. I yelped in panic and saw that worms were dropping down from beneath the dashboard and through the circular ventilation openings. They must be getting into the engine through the radiator grille. I felt worms crawling up my legs and stamped down viciously as I started the engine. The starter whined twice and the engine roared to life. Immediately there was a sickening smell that made me want to retch. I had smelt it before but never so intensely – in the enclosed atmosphere of the car it was insupportable. The stream of worms abated for a few seconds and then a fresh batch appeared from the ventilator opening; it was like watching tubes of meat emerge from a mincing machine. I pulled my legs up on the seat and tried to tuck my trousers into my socks. Any worms that I could feel between trouser and flesh, I crushed to pieces. All the time I knew that I was fighting a losing battle: the worms were coming in faster and I could not block every gap and opening beneath the dashboard. If the engine did not seize up under their weight I would have to cut it or be asphyxiated by their stench.

At this moment I saw two lights ahead. A vehicle was approaching, slowly by the look of it. I switched on the head-lights and dipped them. The patterns of light writhed and shimmered with the weight of worms that were crawling on the glass. I could see through their opaque bodies on the wind-screen as if through a thick blind. I knew this must be my only chance to escape; I sounded my horn and heard an answering blare. My hand moved to the door handle and I temporarily forgot the worms that were clustering round my ankles. The lights came nearer and I waited until they glared large through the windscreen, then I threw my shoulder against the door and sprang out.

CHAPTER THIRTEEN

The moment that I left the car it was as if I had stepped into a living mulch; the worms came above my ankles. I took a step forward, slipped and fell. My hands slid through a mass of slimy bodies and I immediately felt them fasten themselves to every inch of flesh that was presented. Desperately I pulled myself to my knees and staggered towards the vehicle that was nearly on top of me. Once I had got beyond the blinding headlights I recognized Colonel Fraser's Range Rover, its roof piled with coils of barbed wire. A door opened and hands reached out to pull me inside.

'Douse him!' Colonel Fraser was at the wheel wearing military uniform. He began to ease the vehicle forward the minute that I was inside it. There were two men in the back also in army uniform; one of them I recognized from the village. Barely able to conceal their repugnance they began to sponge the exposed parts of my body with a liquid that smelt like petrol. The worms dropped away and in some places I saw that they had left weals which spouted a thin line of blood. The liquid stung but I was grateful to be alive.

'What in God's name is happening?' I asked.

'I think God's name has little to do with it,' said the Colonel grimly. 'We're sealing off the area. Something's gone wrong with the turbine cooling system at the reactors. Meddling scientific morons trying to be too damned clever!' His spittle showed against the windscreen as he craned forward. 'Now they can see what they've done – those of them that are left.'

'I was trying to get to the cottage hospital at Boston Market,' I said. 'Mrs Valentine's cleaning woman has been taken desperately ill. She needs a doctor.'

'You won't find one at Boston Market, or anywhere else for

that matter. All the doctors in the area have been called in to the reactor.' He shook his head vengefully. 'I wish I had that glib swine Brownly in front of me now.'

The man beside me shuddered. 'God knows what they've done.' He plucked a worm from my collar and swore as he smeared it against the seat back. 'This could be only the beginning.'

I looked ahead. The silver tide was still slithering across the road but in reduced numbers. I thought of the Controller's words when he had been smugly telling me how a nuclear reactor had served the needs of the Colchester oyster industry: 'waxed fat and juicy'. At the time the expression had caused me qualms, and now I felt like a man watching a nightmare come to life. By some strange quirk of nature and man's incompetence and hubris all at the same time, one of the lowest forms of life had been reprogrammed into an instrument of mass destruction. 'The worm turns' – what irony could be found in that expression, one of man's simplest servants now becoming his destroyer, not scavenging the meat from his dead bones but eating it live.

'What am I going to do?' I said.

Colonel Fraser began to accelerate as the worms were left behind. Marsh House loomed up in front.

'You'd better get back to Mrs Valentine. Lock yourself in, of course, and seal every opening. As soon as we've established a road barrier and closed off the area I'll try and get somebody to you. Some form of pesticide is on the way – in principle it should see them off.' He slowed down and stopped in front of the drive.

'But Mrs Mullins—?'

Colonel Fraser reached behind him and threw open the door. 'There's six dead men at the reactor and another ten probably going to join them. A doctor will arrive when there's one available.' He gunned the motor impatiently.

'Good look,' said the man beside me. It was the local equivalent of 'goodbye'.

I stepped out onto the wet, glistening road and almost immediately the Range Rover accelerated away, the coils of barbed wire on its roof swaying and creaking. I was terrified and alone. At any moment a flood of worms might come slithering out of the darkness towards me. I listened to the receding sound of the Range Rover engine and started up the drive. I had taken three steps when I heard the screech of brakes and the sound of an impact; as I turned there was another loud noise and then a crack. Then the sound of men shouting in pain and panic. I ran to the road and looked in the direction the Range Rover had taken. A hundred yards away there was what looked like an oil slick in the road and a bicycle sticking out of a ditch, one wheel silhouetted against the night sky. The Range Rover was further down the road; it had crashed into a telegraph pole which was pinning it down like the leg of a crab.

I had run about twenty yards when there was a violent explosion and a jet of flame that shot into the air as from a giant roman candle. The Range Rover had burst into flames and was burning from end to end – whatever Colonel Fraser's men had used to get the worms off me must have been petrol or petrol-based. The flames revealed what had caused the crash. Like a line of marching ants, a dense swathe of worms traversed the road. Shrinking from the heat they fell back on each other in waves like the furled petals of a flower. The flames roared and crackled and drowned the screams of the burning men. I could feel my eyelashes scorching. There was no chance of getting within thirty feet of the blazing wreckage. Even the telegraph pole was alight. I could see a human shape trying to escape through a window and then it was engulfed by flames and disappeared from sight. It was a spectacle so ghastly that I started to cry out aloud, calling God's name repeatedly. What was horrifying was the way that the worms maintained their position round the blaze as if waiting for any human being that emerged from it.

I turned and ran towards the bicycle. Now that I was nearer

I could see the front wheel was buckled; the Range Rover must have hit it before skidding into the telegraph pole. Something about the heavy, old fashioned outline of the bicycle was familiar. I looked along the ditch, horrified of what I might see. Sure enough a column of worms had infiltrated from an adjoining channel. They were clustered thickly about something, something from which a human hand projected. At first I could not recognize the face and then I saw a band of white around the neck. It was the vicar. His head moved slightly and my stomach heaved as I saw that his face was covered in worms; they were entering his mouth and nostrils, probing beneath his eyelids. A darker, jelloid mass hung from his temple and was almost indistinguishable from the worms.

I began to retch and turned to run back towards the house. As I did so I felt a familiar slimy touch against the bare flesh of my ankle. Two files of worms had climbed from the ditch and were surrounding me; their soft bodies crushed beneath my shoes and I almost slipped before leaving them behind and hearing my footsteps echo on the glistening macadam. The light from the still burning Range Rover projected my shadow down the road and I looked like a figure dancing in the flames of hell. In my present situation the comparison hardly seemed an exaggeration of the reality. Marsh House was cut off with the worms on each side of it. Colonel Fraser and his men were dead and there was no contact with the outside world. I remembered what the soldier had said: 'This could be only the beginning.'

I entered the drive and cried out as something dropped onto my neck; it was water dripping from an overhanging branch. I paused to regain my breath and looked about me warily. The glow from the lamp above the porch threw enough light to show that the drive was empty save for Mrs Valentine's car. There was no sign of movement from the adjacent lawn. I controlled my breathing and listened. The silence was ominous: not a rustle, not a breath of wind. I looked behind me nervously and continued to the house. I was about to bang the knocker when I thought of Mrs Mullins; I had left the house to try and find a doctor. Now, four men were dead and I had achieved nothing except the precarious salvation of my own life. Mrs Mullins was no better off for my return. An idea occurred to me: her medicine had been left in the cottage, I could get that – that would be a positive act. I listened again; still the eerie quiet. I imagined the worms slithering through the grass . . . I would have to move fast.

Almost immediately regretting my decision I started off along the gleaming box hedge. Something caught my eye on the path and I sucked in breath. It was a snail. Perhaps sensing an enemy presence in the vibration of my footsteps, it withdrew into its shell. I stamped on it. Ahead, the lights were still on in the cottage; it stood out against the night like a miniature lighthouse. I approached it warily and peered through the window. Everything seemed exactly as it had been left; I could even see the wet slimy stain of spittle that Mrs Mullins had left on the chair back. I went inside and looked around again before crossing to the sink. The tray of bottles had gone. I glanced beside the armchair and then came to the conclusion that Mrs Valentine must have come back to collect the medicine whilst I was away.

I was about to leave when I heard a muffled squeaking noise, like the sound of two balloons being rubbed together. Terrified by what I might see, I looked towards the door that led down to the boathouse. The escutcheon that I had nailed in place was trembling as if something on the other side of the door was trying to work it free. There was a cracking noise and a fissure ran down the top panel of the door, then the whole door flinched. I stood motionless, rooted to the spot. I could scarcely believe what I knew must exist on the other side of that door: the pressure of millions of worms packing every inch of those dark, narrow stairs, worms that had crawled out of the mud from the ditches and the dense reed beds where they had been massing, worms programmed by some avenging force that could surely never reside in heaven.

Then the lights went out. My heart pulsed as if an electric current had been passed through it. There was only the glow of the dying fire behind me; in the faint light the door gleamed and the panels seemed to expand as if they were breathing. There was an explosive cracking noise and the door burst open. A wall of worms poured into the room as if a vast container had split open. I was buried up to my knees and nearly knocked backwards into the fire. There was a hissing sound and the embers were extinguished by a mass of worms that slapped against the base of the chimney. What little light there had been was snuffed out and the room filled with a foul-smelling pungent smoke. I was now struggling in the pitch black amidst a spreading army of writhing worms.

The noise of their slithering bodies filled my ears as I tried to wade towards the door; I could feel them against my bare flesh as they penetrated every opening in my clothing and squirmed towards my face. Once I fell and my face pressed against the obscene slimy carpet, I felt something penetrating my nostril and plucked it out. I wanted to scream but I decided not to open my mouth. I pulled myself up against the armchair and continued to drag my feet towards the door; it was like trying to make progress in a swamp. I seized the door knob and tried to turn it. My hands were slipping too much to get a grip. The level of the worms seemed to be rising; I could feel them round my crutch. I struck out with my fists in a futile gesture born of mounting hysteria; my blows sank into the soft mass as if into jelly. I was achieving nothing save the exhaustion of my fast-fading reserves of strength. I abandoned the door and tore at the window catch. It came free but the frame of the window was jammed; I pressed hard but it would not open. Desperately I threw my fist at it and felt broken glass scarring my knuckles; the window opened half an inch and cold air blew against my cheek. I lashed out again and the window burst open. Immediately I propelled myself forward and felt the metal tooth digging into my belly as I sprawled across the sill. The worms were like suction pads securing my feet but I dragged myself free and toppled into a flowerbed minus a shoe. The damp earth pressed against my face and I clawed myself to my feet, not knowing whether I would find the garden over-run with worms.

Still panic-stricken I staggered away from the cottage and started to run towards the house. It was pitch black and a branch stung me across the face. I blundered into the box hedge and ripped my hands on a rose bower. Now I could see the house before me and the deep rectangles of curtained light. I arrived at the front door and banged savagely on the knocker. Behind me the shadows lapped against the pool of light cast by the lamp above the porch; with every second that passed I expected to see the worms pursuing me from the darkness. I banged again and the door opened unexpectedly, almost projecting me into the house. I staggered into the warm hall feeling a momentary pang of relief.

Little did I know it then but the worst part of my ordeal was just beginning.

CHAPTER FOURTEEN

I stood in the hall gasping for breath and winced as I saw my reflection in the mirror. I looked about twenty years older than my true age; my flesh was grey and sagged in dark pouches under my fear-crazed eyes; my hair was bedraggled and my nose bleeding. My hands and face were scratched and covered with a film of mucous-like slime which also festooned my clothing. My body was literally crawling with worms, some of which materialized from my clothing to drop to the floor and wriggle away towards new hiding places.

Beside me, Mrs Valentine shrank back, her face registering shock and disgust. For several seconds neither of us spoke. 'What happened?' she asked at length.

As quickly as I could, I described what had taken place since I left the house: the disaster at the nuclear reactor and its effect on the worms. 'At any moment they're going to come here,' I told her. 'Somehow we've got to try and keep them out. How's Mrs Mullins?'

'Very ill – I don't think she's got much longer.' Mrs Valentine looked round the hall as if wondering what to do next. I think she was as bemused as I was: what we were experiencing defied comprehension.

'We must try and close up every hole they might get through,' I said. 'Do you have shutters?'

As I spoke I tore off my coat and jacket. The squirming of the worms was driving me mad. Mrs Valentine looked down at the writhing shapes with an expression of fascinated horror. 'Poor Colonel Fraser. Are you certain he's dead?'

'We'll all be dead if we don't do something,' I said. I went into the dining room and found Mrs Mullins lying where I had left her; her skin was dark grey but she was still breathing fitfully. Mrs Valentine appeared beside me. 'You collected the medicine?' I asked her.

She hesitated slightly. 'Er . . . yes – but I think she may be past medicines though.' I detected a certain acceptance in the voice that was only a shade away from satisfaction. I glanced at her; she was looking down at Mrs Mullins's inert body with an expression that showed no trace of compassion. A fresh feeling of unease and uncertainty began to cloud my mind.

A noise from outside brought me back to a realization of the immediate danger. I told Mrs Valentine to lay her hands on any candles that were in the house and went round checking that all the windows were closed and locked. After my experience at the cottage I had little confidence that this measure would keep the worms at bay, but it was necessary to go through the motions of taking every basic precaution. In each room that I entered I pressed the tip of my nose against the cold window panes and peered out into the garden. There was no sign of movement. The grass glistened and there was an occasional patch of melting snow. The only shapes were large familiar ones: bushes, rose beds, a garden seat.

I went back to the drawing room. Mrs Valentine rose from Mrs Mullins's side. 'How is she?' I asked.

'The same.'

'There's nothing we can do?' Mrs Valentine shook her head resignedly. 'The telephone's still not working?'

'It wasn't five minutes ago.'

I went into the hall and lifted the receiver – the line was still dead. I looked towards the front door; there was a large opening for letters. I fetched a hefty piece of kindling from the log basket and wedged it shut. Mrs Valentine was watching me all the time as a child might watch a carpenter at work. I looked up the long flight of stairs. 'What about the rest of the house?'

She looked at me incredulously. 'Surely they can't . . .' Her voice trailed away as if she found the idea too unbelievable.

'When they come they can go anywhere. I'd like to get an idea of the layout of the house.' I did not wait for a reply but picked up one of the candles that had been left burning in the hall; I did not want to be left in the dark again if the lights suddenly went out.

'I'll show you.' Mrs Valentine led the way upstairs and along a corridor throwing open the doors on each side as we went past. I noticed that she and her husband appeared to have had separate bedrooms with a dressing room and bathroom suite in between. We went past a narrow flight of stairs leading upwards and I stopped.

'What's up there?'

'The attics.' She started back down the corridor as if eager that we should move on. I hesitated and then followed her. 'May I suggest that you have a bath?' she said. 'I think you might find that some of my husband's clothes would fit you. You must be terribly uncomfortable like that.'

She was right. I still had a number of worms about my person that were making their presence felt. The nauseating slime that had attached itself to my face, hands and clothing was also congealing and sticking to every surface that I touched; I dared not think what I must smell like. Was it safe to take a bath? We must have some notice if the worms attacked.

'Thank you,' I said. 'I would like a quick bath.'

She showed me a wardrobe full of suits and indicated a chest of drawers in which she said that I should find all the other clothes I needed. I thanked her and told her to shout if anything happened. The bathroom was next to the dressing-room and the moment she had gone I climbed into the bath and started to peel off my clothes. Soon I was naked and the bath was crawling with writhing shapes wriggling for cover beneath my discarded clothes. Making sure that there were no more worms attached to me I stepped out of the bath and turned on the hot tap. For a terrifying second I thought a stream of worms would pour out but there was only boiling hot water. With grim satisfaction I watched the worms bleached into strips of white ribbon and flushed down the plug hole. When the last pocket had been turned inside out and the last worm scalded to oblivion, I ran in some cold water and rinsed and wrung my clothing more or less dry. I draped it across a towel rail and ran myself a hot bath, pressing down the plug with every ounce of strength that I still possessed.

The feel of hot, clean water against my flesh was a balm but I was in no condition to take full advantage of it. With every second that passed I expected to hear a scream from below, or see some other manifestation of the worms' presence. I scrubbed myself clean and quickly dried myself with a thick bath towel. One worm had somehow managed to survive the hot water and was crawling down the arm of my suit. I picked up a soap dish and crushed it to pieces.

Satisfied that everything was as it should be, I pressed home the plug in the wash basin and went into the dressing-room. The late Mr Valentine had certainly been well endowed with clothes, though his wife had flattered me when she suggested that we might be about the same size; he had clearly been a larger man than me. I selected a pair of trousers and a pair of shoes and started going through the chest of drawers that Mrs Valentine had indicated.

Socks and underclothes were no problem and I pulled open a drawer looking for a shirt. Three neatly folded piles of them met my eye. I selected one and felt my fingers brush against something; it proved to be a mounted photograph which showed a face I recognized – that of the effigy of Sir Robert de Wicklem. The photograph must have been taken in Blanely Church. The face was gazing serenely skywards, the eyelids closed. What was remarkable, however, was that there was another profile beside it and not that of Sir Robert's wife. With a sharp intake of breath I realized where I had seen the face before: it was Edgar Valentine, Mrs Valentine's dead husband, whose portrait I had seen in the drawing room downstairs. I was no expert on photography but it did not look as if the second image had been superimposed on a photograph of the first, so I had been right: the photograph had certainly been taken in the church. It seemed a macabre idea, although the

resemblance between de Wicklem and Valentine was aston-
ishing. I wondered if the vicar had known about this and then
remembered that he had not come to the parish until after
Edgar Valentine's death. I recalled that the body had never
been found and experienced a new tinge of unease. Could
Edgar Valentine actually have been dead when this photograph was taken? His eyelids were closed and there was no
hint of clothing on the upper part of his body. It was a chilling
thought and I looked around the room, almost expecting to
see him emerge from a cupboard. Did Mrs Valentine know
about this photograph? She must do since she had presumably
packed away all her husband's effects after his death. I put the
photograph back in the drawer and slid it shut. I had undone
the third button on the shirt when another thought occurred
to me: perhaps Mrs Valentine had taken the photograph.

There was a sharp tap on the door that made me jump. 'I've
made some tea. It's downstairs when you're ready. Would you
like some cake?'

I was famished and I said I would. I finished dressing and
rather self-consciously went downstairs to the drawing room.
Mrs Mullins was where we had left her, but I had the impression that Mrs Valentine had done something to her hair. She
smiled at me and patted the sofa beside her. 'Do you take
sugar? I can't remember.'

I said that I did and sat on the sofa. I felt thoroughly confused; there were so many things happening that defied
logical explanation. Mrs Valentine's expression was calmness
personified. 'That pullover looks so much better on you than it
did on Edgar.' She was pouring the tea as she spoke. Her hand
did not flinch.

'I only heard recently about his tragic death,' I said. 'I'm
sorry. It must have been terrible for you.'

Her eyes rose to the portrait of her late husband above the
fire; without looking from it she handed me my tea. 'I never
realized how terrible.' Her voice was suddenly heavy and expres-
sionless as if her own personality had been taken away from it.

'I know, it's difficult adjusting to being on your own, isn't it?' I sipped the tea and walked to the nearest window. I pulled back the curtain quickly, holding my breath. There was nothing to be seen.

'He was a strange man.' Mrs Valentine continued to speak in the same disembodied voice. 'There was so much good in him.'

I glanced towards the fireplace and Mrs Mullins. Small white bubbles started to appear at the corner of her mouth, and at the same instant her eyes opened wide in an expression of terror. She was looking straight at me and for some inexplicable reason I read a message of warning in her piercing glance. At first I thought it was levelled at the cup that I was raising to my lips. Unnerved, I replaced it on the circular silver tray, next to a plate of what looked like home-made cakes. I resisted taking one. Mrs Valentine was gazing into space. 'If he had been less admirable I would never have submitted to his wishes.' She suddenly turned to me. 'I thought it was just a weakness, you see. If I pandered to it, everything else would be all right.' I nodded, trying to focus on what she was saying; my attention was still half taken up with the dying woman by the fireplace.

Mrs Mullins's mouth started to open and her lips pulled apart strips of saliva. I waited for the words that did not come. Her head nodded forward and her eyes opened even wider; inside her was a message she could not deliver. Her head jerked forward again. Then I realized what she was trying to say. She was telling me to look behind me.

I turned my head and cried out in horror. Gleaming against one of the windows where the curtains were not properly drawn was a waving mass of worms. They clung to the pane and their heads swayed from side to side as if they were probing for an opening. Mrs Valentine sprang to her feet and together we approached the window. Hardly had we time to see that it was safely closed than there was the crash of breaking glass behind us. I spun round to find a curtain billowing away from another window as if thrust back with a lance. A cluster of writhing worms dropped to the floor. As the curtain fell aside, I saw what at first glance seemed like the black foliated antennae of a giant insect protruding through a broken pane of glass. Then I saw that it was the branch of a monkey puzzle tree on which the worms had clustered in such numbers as to force it through the window. Within a couple of seconds the foliage of the branch became unrecognizable under the weight of the invading worms. Mrs Valentine's expression revealed panic and amazement; I doubt if, until that moment, she had completely believed my story. There was a shattering noise from another part of the house and I ran to see what had happened. At least the lights were still on. I arrived at the inner door of the conservatory and saw that the worms had overbalanced a bird table and forced it to crash through the glass too. It occurred to me that it was not just their concentrated weight that they could use but their excavating skills; in sufficient numbers they were capable of undermining any structure.

The tiled floor of the conservatory was already a squirming sea of pink and I noticed that smaller numbers of worms were entering through the openings in rotted window frames and faulty closures. In an old house like this there was no way of keeping the worms at bay; every crack and cranny that would let in a draught would let in a worm. I ran to the back of the house and saw that worms were coming in beneath the kitchen door and in even greater numbers through the damp courses. The speed of their build-up was terrifying. Flood water could scarcely have spread faster or been more impossible to control. I was already treading them underfoot as I returned to Mrs Valentine, who was in the hall holding a bundle of candles. 'I can't believe it,' she shuddered. 'I think I must be going mad.'

'You go upstairs,' I told her. 'I'll try and bring Mrs Mullins.'

'No!' She suddenly gripped my arm hard. 'Leave her. She's as good as dead.'

I thought at first that her concern must be directed at me.
'We can't abandon her,' I said.

'Yes! She is an evil, wicked woman. This is God's will.' The
expression on her face was so intense as to be frightening.
shook myself free of her arm and entered the drawing room.
If I had wanted to save Mrs Mullins I was already too late;
her features were unrecognizable under a seething mass of
worms. Her body was a moving mound. The writhing carpet
was quickly unrolling across the rest of the room towards the
doorway. I looked up at the portrait above the chimneypiece;
perhaps it was the reflection of the light but Edgar Valentine
appeared to be smiling. I turned away from the horrible sight
and felt something cold and clammy against my ankle. A trail
of worms led to the front door where they had found a way
through beneath the lowest hinge. I took the candle from the
hall table and started up the staircase to where Mrs Valentine
stood. 'You see?' she said. 'There was nothing we could do.'
She was white but composed.

I did not answer but looked down the stairs behind me. The
trail of worms from the front door had joined that from the
drawing room; they were converging on the staircase. 'We
must go to the attic,' I said. 'I imagine there's only one opening
to the rest of the house?'

'Yes.' Her voice had a quality of resignation about it, I
observed amid a confusion of other thoughts. I remembered
how she had hurried past the staircase leading to the attic
on our tour. Why had she described Mrs Mullins as an 'evil,
wicked woman'? There was certainly something bizarre and
frightening about Mrs Valentine that I had never noticed
before.

My shoulders brushed against the side of the attic staircase
and the boards creaked underfoot. A sharp turn and a steep
rise brought me face to face with a latched door. I pressed
the catch and had just stooped to enter when the lights went
out. Lit only by candlelight, our surroundings seemed doubly
claustrophobic and menacing. I pushed open the door and

was relieved to feel it scraping against the floor; the tighter
its fit the better, I thought, pushing it closed again, although
I knew from my experience at the cottage that it would only
be a matter of time before the worms breached it. However,
time might be of the essence. Colonel Fraser had spoken of a
pesticide that was being sought for use against the worms; if
we could hold out until this was procured then we might have
a chance.

With stooped shoulders I advanced to the centre of the attic
where I could stand without discomfort. There was a skylight
through which I could see stars and two large water tanks.
Pipes, some of them lagged, curved round the floor at knee
height. It was very cold. My eyes began to grow accustomed
to the gloom and I placed my candle on a beam. One side of
the attic was packed tight with dust-covered furniture and I
selected a small marble-topped dressing table and dragged
it to the door. Mrs Valentine expressed no surprise when I
braced it against the door and piled every object within reach
on top of it.

'This is so ghastly,' she said. She sounded as if she was
talking to herself.

I picked up one of a line of paintings propped against
the wall and paused; at first I thought that the haughty man
depicted was Edgar Valentine but the side whiskers and cravat
spoke of an earlier era. What caught my eye was the coat of
arms prominently displayed beside the head. In the bottom
left-hand quarter was the insignia that I had seen on the tomb
of Sir Robert de Wicklem in Blanely Church. 'Who is this?' I
asked.

'Edgar's father.'

I looked back at the coat of arms and suddenly felt the
same chill that I had experienced in Blanely church. 'So you
mean that your husband was a descendant of Sir Robert de
Wicklem?'

Mrs Valentine nodded. 'That's where it came from, the evil
that was in him.' She gestured with her hands. 'It pains me to

think about it but there was a side of him that was depraved. In the building where you now live he would forge objects of metal with which to pinion and abuse me. He would snare birds, and decorate me with their bloody feathers before he—' She shuddered and shook her head as if the truth was too horrible to repeat.

I knew that I stood poised on the threshold of further revelations. 'What about Mrs Mullins?' I asked, suddenly convinced I was about to understand the mystery of the silver teaspoons.

'She was a part of it all. First Edgar made me submit to the gardener whilst he watched, then the Mullins woman was brought into it. The vile soon became commonplace. Each new excess had to be worse than the last. Even the setting.'

'The church,' I said, thinking of the photograph I had found in the drawer.

She nodded. 'That was the last straw.'

'So you killed him,' I said.

A note of wariness entered Mrs Valentine's voice. 'His boat was found off the point. It was empty.' She sounded as if she was reading from a newspaper report. I waited for her to continue.

'With Edgar's death I thought I was free. Then came the blackmail. Wilson and Betty Mullins . . . They had some photographs.'

As I listened I understood why she had lied to protect Mrs Mullins in the affair of the teaspoons; she had known that the woman was stealing but dared not say anything.

I thought I heard something pressing against the door and hurried to it with one of the candles. I was trembling. Everything she had said reinforced the terrible evil of the place. I passed the candle around the outside of the door. There was nothing to be seen.

I turned and found Mrs Valentine standing in front of me, the ivory letter opener in her hand. It was pressed against her lower abdomen with the blade pointing upwards. Her fingertips brushed against it. 'I think we are two of a kind, you and I,' she said. My blood ran cold. What did she know? She smiled at me mockingly. 'Wilson told me that he overheard you having an argument with your wife. She didn't want to come and live here, did she?' I said nothing; I could feel the prickling of cold sweat on my forehead. Had I survived so much to be once again at the mercy of another human being?

Mrs Valentine took a step towards me so that our bodies were almost touching. 'Tell me the truth.' She smiled again, and in the half light her face looked as soft and appealing as it must have done twenty years before. With a shudder of distaste it occurred to me that the sexual degradation she had suffered at the hands of her husband might not have been as repugnant to her as she laid claim. Either that or she had been thoroughly corrupted almost without her knowing. I tried to draw back but she followed me. Her face was close to mine; there was a soft fuzz on her cheek like that on a peach. Her lips were full and sensual. She must have been very beautiful when she was young, young and innocent.

'What did you do to your wife?' she murmured softly. 'Did you push the concrete onto her?' The words struck me as if they had been a blow across the face. I brought up my hands and thrust my persecutor back against one of the water tanks. She threw out an arm to save herself and for an instant it hovered above the tank; she snatched it away and I caught a look of real fear in her eyes. It was as if there was something in the tank that she would rather have died than touch. Icy fingers of terror traced a path down my spine but I was unable to restrain myself. Steeling myself, I walked slowly towards the tank and peered over the edge.

What I saw froze the cry of terror in my throat. A shrivelled body stared up at me through eyeless sockets. A parchment skin clung to the top of the head but the rest of the face was a skull with a nasal cavity and two rows of grinning teeth; swollen papier mâché fingers protruded from the sleeves of a dust-impregnated dinner jacket, and the mummified flesh was pock-marked with worm holes. I stood silent with revulsion, knowing that I was looking down upon Edgar Valentine and that he had died by the hand of his wife who was standing but a few feet away from me.

I jerked my head away and turned to Mrs Valentine. Her eyes were wide and her fingers tightened around the knife. My heart was thumping so hard that it seemed about to leap from my body. And then I heard the noise. Like a wet finger being drawn across a window pane. I looked up and saw a coiling mass of worms spilling across the skylight above my head. Pressed against the glass the worms turned it into a mirror and I found myself staring at the terrifying apparition of Edgar Valentine's corpse which lay below. It was as if the top had been prised off a tomb and a long-interred body revealed.

Paralysed with fear, unable to speak, I returned my gaze to Mrs Valentine. Her lips parted in a chilling smile and she slowly raised her arm. She was going to stab me. I knew it, yet I was unable to move. The corners of her mouth tightened and she took a step towards me. I opened my mouth to cry out and no sound came. At that instant the skylight shattered under the weight of the worms. The broken frame fell on Mrs Valentine and a squirming mass of worms dropped into the tank and landed on my head and shoulders. I could feel them wriggling in my hair. My face was cut by broken glass. I flung myself to one side and saw Mrs Valentine tottering before me, her hand pressed to her neck and blood spurting through her fingers. A splinter of glass protruded grotesquely from her neck. Her mouth opened and blood gushed from it. Worms thudded to the floor as they continued to surge through the shattered skylight. Mrs Valentine let out a ghastly choking cry that seemed to pour from the depths of her throat like vomit and fell to her knees.

Gibbering with terror I tried to shake the first invading mass free of my legs and ran across the room to the door. Whatever lay beyond it I knew that if I stayed in the attic any longer I would go out of my mind. I hurled the table aside and caught a glimpse of Edgar Valentine's father as the glass splintered across his portrait. For the first time it occurred to me that the reversed half circles on the de Wicklem coat of arms were like wriggling worms. I pulled open the door and a tidal wave of worms spilled into the room. By what little light reached me from the candle on the beam I could see a glistening trail stretching down the stairs like one long moving serpent. I launched myself forward and half fell, half slid down the mulch of bodies. The corridor when I reached it was infested with them and already I could feel them everywhere against my bare flesh: beneath my arms, my genitals, probing between the cleft of my buttocks, stretching out for my ears, my mouth, my nostrils – I was plucking handfuls of them away from my face. And all this in reeking darkness. No words come to my mind with which I can adequately describe their stench. God knows what had passed through their bodies.

I blundered into a bedroom and crushed the door shut against their vile softness. I had no idea where I was going or what I was looking for. In the room there was a faint glow of moonlight reflected from a white counterpane. A fire had been laid in the grate and near it was what, in my half-crazed state, I first took for a coiled snake. As I stared closer I saw that it was a gas poker. Desperately I slapped my body for matches; I had neither matches nor lighter. Worms were already flooding under the door like a sea of blood. I searched the mantelpiece and found a round glass jar with corrugated sides that contained matches. With fumbling fingers I brushed worms away from my face and struck one, spilling the rest across the floor. I dropped to my knees and fumbled with the gas tap. As the gas came on with a comforting hiss, the match went out. I had to scramble about in the darkness for another, my fingers already meeting the squirming horror of the advancing worms. My hands were slimy and for a few terrifying seconds I found it impossible to strike a match. Then one flared briefly and the poker burst into flame. All along its length bright tongues of fire leapt out. I dropped to my knees and, holding it just above floor level, swept it from side to side. Any worms in its path were scorched to charred smears. The remainder held their distance and formed a threatening half circle that stretched around the fireplace, just as they had done when the Range Rover had been burning. The number of worms was building up all the time and sometimes a wave would be forced forward, stopping only when I plunged the poker into it so deep that the flames were almost invisible. Then there would be an obscene crackling noise and a whiff of foul, choking smoke, a bubbling jelly of congealed slime and a whiplash of half-burnt bodies thrashing in their death agonies. Did worms feel pain? I hoped so as I burned them. I had seen them dance on a fisherman's hook and felt compassion; now I felt only loathing and a desire for revenge.

I swung the poker again and suddenly saw something burning out of the corner of my eye. One of the curtains was smouldering. As I hesitated, wondering what to do, it burst into flames that reached to the pelmet. In no time the panelling was alight. I tore the blazing curtain down and threw it on the worms. Desperate, I pulled the window open and immediately the flames rose higher, fanned by the draught, the heat scorching my arms. Behind me the worms shrank back. I looked out of the window; it was twenty feet to the ground, perhaps more. Nearby, an ancient wisteria twisted its way up the side of the house. Some burning material fell across my shoulders and I screamed out in pain. The carpet was beginning to burn where I had dropped the poker. I reached out into the night and grabbed the nearest loop of wisteria. At the back of my mind was the thought that if I could reach Mrs Valentine's car then I might be able to drive to some temporary or permanent sanctuary.

The wisteria rustled and branches brushed against my face. One of the supports that held it to the wall quivered menacingly and a sprinkling of ancient mortar pattered to the wet earth below. I hesitated, and then felt my shoulder starting to burn. That was the incentive I needed. I launched myself over the sill and consigned my whole weight to the creeper. It swayed away from the house and then swung back. Barely able to support myself, I struggled to find a foothold and slithered down a couple of feet, scraping my face against some nails in the trellis-work. The wisteria swayed again and this time did not swing back; there was a cracking noise and I found myself supine on the lawn with every ounce of breath driven from me. In considerable pain I struggled out from beneath the serpentine coils of the creeper and raised myself to my feet. At least I had escaped the choking smell, and I could see no worms in the immediate vicinity. All that was visible through the window of the room I had just vacated was a wall of flame – the house was on fire. I did not stay to watch but ran back into the shadows of the garden, intending to take a wide circle to the car and hoping to avoid any worms advancing on the house.

I pushed my way through the wet foliage and the flower-beds, suspicious of every soft pressure underfoot, and followed the outside wall round to the drive. The laurels gleamed and I could see smoke and flames against the night sky. The fire was spreading. I advanced up the drive and nervously approached Mrs Valentine's car. A chance conversation had revealed that she kept a spare ignition key sellotaped to the top of the glove compartment. I looked around for one of the heavy white-washed stones that lined the drive; if the doors were locked I would have to smash my way into the car quickly. I felt the stone between my hands and suddenly thought of Mrs Valentine and what I had left behind in the attic. The clouds of panic parted temporarily and I watched flames begin to stab through the roof. Thank God that I had accidentally set fire to the house; anything that remained of the bodies within would tell no secrets. I tucked the rock under my arm and approached the car almost on tiptoe. There was a foul stench in the air which I knew must be the burning worms. I laid a nervous hand on the door handle and pulled; to my relief it opened. I discarded the stone and ducked inside. Immediately I sprang back. The interior of the car was packed with worms;

they reared up from every surface as if they had been waiting for me. I could no more have climbed into that car than into my own coffin. I turned on my heel and found that a tide of retreating worms was pouring out of the front door of the house. As if my appearance lent them a new momentum they changed direction and spread out towards me.

Now in a state of total panic I burst through the laurels and across the lawn. I had no idea where I was running to. All I wanted to do was to put as much distance between myself and Marsh House as possible. I reached the flint wall and hauled the upper half of my body across it. I was nearly exhausted but fear lent me just enough strength to drag up the weight of my legs and topple over the other side. I landed in a ditch . . . a ditch full of worms.

I slid down amongst them like a plummet into soft mud. They were above my knees, my hips, my waist. Wriggling, writhing, squirming. I screamed until it seemed my lungs must burst. I was still sinking. They were above my chest – in a few moments they would be in my mouth. Ahead I saw a line of lights and heard the roar of engines; something was approaching across the marsh. Was it real or was I imagining it? The lights were red and spaced out. I suddenly realized that they must be on the wings of planes flying low across the marshes. My mouth dipped below the surface of the writhing bodies and I spat out with all my remaining force. A worm was insinuating itself into the back of the nostril and I plucked at it desperately; only half of its body came away. I sneezed and tried to snort away the remaining half. Eventually I swallowed it. The engine noise became deafening and the lights swooped low overhead. The grass shook and something that burned like acid stung my face. The planes were spraying the worms. As I choked, the activity of the worms about me became feverish and then suddenly slackened. I could feel death permeating through them layer by layer. In less than sixty seconds I was imprisoned not by writhing bodies but by a dense comatose mass. I might have been trapped in a thick swamp. Slowly, inch by inch, I dragged myself to the bank and pulled myself up it with the aid of tussocks of grass. Around me there was no sight or sound of movement save the distant roar of the sea. There was only the smell of the insecticide and, increasingly, of the dead worms. It was cold but I was now hardly aware of physical discomfort. I collapsed by the side of the road and that is where they found me.

CHAPTER FIFTEEN

If anything ever appeared in the national newspapers concerning the invasion of the worms then I never saw it. Mind you, it was difficult enough to find a national newspaper in Blanely for several weeks after the onslaught, because the whole area remained sealed off. I think the official reason was that a freak storm had devastated the region. In fact piles of rotting worms were being sprayed, burned and buried in giant pits. The bulldozers worked twenty-four hours a day and you could see their headlights across the marshes at night. What was happening at the reactor was more of a secret: something had obviously gone seriously wrong and nobody was allowed within two miles of it. 'Counsellors' appeared in the village to hold what were called 'clarification sessions' for the inhabitants and it was explained that we had witnessed an unusual but entirely natural phenomenon which would never occur again; to relate it to the 'explosion' at the reactor would be totally erroneous and in fact against the public interest. We were all asked to sign a piece of paper to the effect that we understood this and would not make any inflammatory statements to the press or anyone else which might provide ammunition for our country's enemies. We were further informed that the area had been ear-marked for a large beet-processing plant which would provide a great deal of employment for local people both in its building and staffing. As a special dispensation, the government had also decided to make generous pension settlements on the relatives of those who had perished in the 'storm'. I could see people sitting at the meeting and beginning to believe what they were told and not what they had seen. Spring was coming and everything would look better when there was some blossom on the trees.

In fact, spring had come when, one sunny morning, there was a brisk tap on the door of my cottage. I opened it and saw two men I had never seen before. They were middle-aged and wore slate-grey raincoats. They nodded perfunctorily and one of them withdrew a polythene-covered card which he flashed before my eyes.

'Mr Hildebrand? C.I.D. I wonder if we could have a few words with you.' They stepped over the threshold as if a negative reply was unthinkable.

I had always been nervous of the police and nothing that had happened in the last few months had made me any less so.

'More questions?' I said. 'I thought everything had been tidied up.'

'Something's just come to light,' said the elder of the two men. 'It relates to Mrs Betty Mullins.'

I immediately felt relieved. If it had been about Mrs Valentine I would have been more worried. Despite the fact that only her charred remains had been found I still feared that some brilliant forensic specialist at Scotland Yard might find evidence of her neck wound that could raise their suspicions against me.

'Oh, yes. Poor Mrs Mullins,' I murmured.

'Did you know that she had been poisoned?'

The silence lasted several seconds. The second detective removed a small pad from his pocket and licked the tip of his thumb.

'Poisoned?' I stammered.

The first detective nodded briefly. 'Yes. We've just had the report in. As you know, the fire hardly touched the lower part of the house. Her body was recovered more or less intact apart from what the worms had done to it. In the labs they found that all the worms in her stomach were dead – poisoned. The body was riddled with it.'

'How terrible,' I said. 'Of course, I knew nothing about this. Did she try to kill herself?'

'If she did, she chose to do it very slowly. The report states that the intake of poison had been small and spread over a period of weeks. That's hardly usual in a suicide.'

'No,' I said. I thought of the slow deterioration in Mrs Mullins's health and of the expression in Mrs Valentine's eyes as she looked down at her in the drawing room. Mrs Valentine must have done it. No wonder Mrs Mullins had fought against the administration of the medicine that day in my cottage; she must have realized what was happening to her: the age-old remedy for blackmailers. I remembered Wilson doubling up in his cottage before I had killed him. Had Mrs Valentine been poisoning him too?

'You'll have no objection if we look around?' I hesitated before answering because I was still thinking about Wilson. The detective produced a piece of paper from his inside jacket pocket. 'We do have a search warrant.'

I felt a chill. 'That's not necessary. You can go anywhere you like.' They must suspect me: that was alarming ... alarming but no more. I was innocent of any crime against Mrs Mullins. True, I had fed her the medicine that had helped to kill her but I had done it in good faith. Anyway, the medicine was not here. It was – my thought process was brought to a sharp halt as I saw the second detective pulling on a pair of gloves. He looked at me meaningfully and reached inside the cupboard beside the sink. What he withdrew made my blood run cold: it was the tray of medicine bottles which Mrs Valentine had brought to the house and which she told me she had removed.

The detective carefully removed one of the stoppers and sniffed. His nose wrinkled. 'What's this, sir?' The 'sir' had a chilling ring to it.

'It's the medicine Mrs Valentine used to give Mrs Mullins.'

'What's it doing here, sir?'

'Mrs Valentine brought it here when Mrs Mullins was suddenly taken ill.'

'And she left it here?' The tone was incredulous.

'She told me she took it away. It was the night of the—' I

paused and then chose the official word; 'it was the night of the storm.'

Suddenly I realized what had happened: why Mrs Valentine had brought the bottles on a tray; why she had asked me to look for one with a green sticker on the bottom; why it was I who administered the medicine. It was so that my fingerprints would be on the bottles and on the spoon. I remembered her peeling off her gloves after she had placed the tray near the sink. How clever she had been. I would guarantee that there would be none of her fingerprints on the bottles. I also knew what was in them: poison.

'Well, sir,' said the elder detective. 'There's just a few formalities. We'll need to take your fingerprints first of all.'

And that is how I come to the end of my narrative. Arrested and imprisoned for a crime I did not commit.

There is perhaps one other detail of the affair that is worth relating. Shortly after the Blanely area was declared 'clean', a baby in its pram was pecked to death by a flock of birds at Great Yarmouth, down the coast. Other attacks on animals and humans were reported in the papers. They appeared to be becoming more frequent at the time of my arrest, and over a much wider area than the worms could ever cover. It was happening all over again.